unWANTED: HUSBAND

unWANTED: HUSBAND

•

Sandra D. Bricker

AVALON BOOKS
NEW YORK

PRINTED IN THE UNITED STATES OF AMERICA
ON ACID-FREE PAPER
BY HADDON CRAFTSMEN, BLOOMSBURG, PENNSYLVANIA

For my good luck charm.
I love you, Mom.

And special thanks to my editor,
Erin Cartwright,
a sassy little romance novel heroine
just waiting to happen.

And to my local Tampa "Tag Team"
of typists & cheerleaders.
Especially Laura, Bruce & Carol.

Chapter One

Wanted: SWM Professional with an eye
for a bargain. Must love to travel and
enjoy being single. Want to experience
everything this world has to offer?
Then this is the ad to answer!

Charlotte Dennison eyed the note curiously for a long
moment where it stood tucked between the home and bottom rows of keys on her keyboard. It finally began to make
sense in a slow pattern that felt like warm molasses dripping from the top of her head. A smile crept across her
face as she closed her hazel eyes and shook her head.

"Great idea, huh?" said a voice behind her.

"Lorette, you are unbelievable, do you know that?" she
cried, the slightest trace of Southern accent resonating in
her voice, her eyes still wrinkled shut.

"Why not?"

Charlotte turned slowly toward her friend and pursed her full lips. Lorette had to be kidding.

"You said you were never getting married again, right?" Lorette waited only a moment for an answer, then moved on, ignoring the icy stare that met her hare-brained idea. "And you said you need to make some more money, right?" Still nothing. "Well, why not?"

"Why not?" Charlotte couldn't help but chuckle. "Why not?"

"Char, it makes perfect sense."

Charlotte wanted to get angry. Anyone else who pushed an idea so hard despite her obvious refusal to even consider it would have evoked that very response. But this was Lorette. She could always get away with what no one else could. And the frustrating part was—Lorette knew it.

"Look," Lorette continued, "it's not as if you'd be fouling up for later. You said your future doesn't hold a partner! And you wouldn't be living under the same roof or anything."

Charlotte tugged the oversized leather bag from beneath her desk and glanced around at the sea of faces before her, all of them crowned in identical headsets, plugged into telephones.

The Reservations floor held nearly four hundred steel-box desks just like hers, and Charlotte could easily remember her first days at Global Airlines when she could barely remember which one was hers. Now, a year later, she could find it blindfolded in the pitch dark.

"You could end up meeting someone fabulous," Lorette teased, and Charlotte tried to ignore the preposterous ramblings, stuffing her belongings into the leather bag and cleaning up the area around her computer.

"I thought the idea wasn't to meet someone fabulous," she replied as she busily moved about. "I thought it wasn't even about romance or love. Just a business proposition. Isn't that what you said three hours ago when all this nonsense began?"

"It isn't nonsense," her friend insisted. "Just think about it."

Charlotte had considered it—for about half a minute. The idea originated amidst casual conversation about a more secure future for both Charlotte and her father. The burden of the monthly increase at the nursing home was weighing heavily on Charlotte's mind, and Lorette had sensed her anxiety. For an instant, the plan almost seemed feasible. Marry someone who needed unlimited air travel. In return, a paltry $750 a month—although Lorette had been pushing for $1,000—and no emotional strings attached. Separate residences. Separate lives.

Charlotte had vowed never to marry again, after a three-year fiasco with Luke, her French ex-husband. He'd moved the last of just a car's trunk full of boxes from their tiny apartment, and all traces of their life together went with him that day.

"Lord," Charlotte had prayed as she watched him drive away, "don't ever let me be so blind again."

And He hadn't. In fact, it had become increasingly evident to Charlotte that destiny's plan for her was solitude. There would be no more room for heartache brought on by bad decisions if she simply had no decisions to make. And Luke had been a mistake committed in her usual trap—haste.

She'd been so sure that he'd been *The One*—her lifelong love. Her mistake proved that she had no sense about such things. Now it was simple. There would be no men after him.

Luke was an artist. It was so romantic—for the first year. Until "the artist" stopped painting, sculpting, and sketching, and began watching the soaps instead. Charlotte would come home with tales of irate customers and huge sales at the cosmetics counter where she worked at the time, and Luke would, in turn, fill her in on all the mischief Erica Kane had been up to on "All My Children."

When it was finally over, Charlotte had toasted her divorce papers with an entire cheesecake, a six-pack of Diet Coke, and the consequential four-day caffeine hangover. Then came the subsequent career change to a job as a Reservations operator at Global Airlines, where she met her dearest friend, Lorette.

The two women were complete opposites; still they found something in each other that laid the foundation for a friendship Charlotte had come to cherish, even depend upon. During the four weeks of computer classes and reservations training, they had become fast friends.

She studied her friend, ignoring the stream of one-track chatter that flowed from her like an unstoppable raft charging down the rapids. Her dark chocolate skin gleamed beneath thin locks of perfect cocoa braids that ran halfway down her back. She looked absolutely beautiful just then in the colorful garb her husband had brought back from his latest trip to Africa.

The oranges and rusts looked lovely against Lorette's skin, and Charlotte thought that she could never carry off wearing such bold colors herself. Not just because Lorette was a beautiful African-American woman, but because she had such a wonderful sense of style. It was all her own, exclusively Lorette.

Charlotte punched in the code to access her voice mail and cringed as she listened to the only message that played back.

"Miss Dennison, we simply must hear back from you about your plans for your father. As you know, the rate increase is effective the first of the month and, if you're planning to make other arrangements, well, there is quite a long waiting list for our facility, and ..."

Charlotte pumped the erase button in frustration without indulging the message to the end.

"Are you listening to me?"

"No, not really," Charlotte replied honestly, then shot Lorette a quick grin as she snatched the piece of paper from her keyboard and wadded it up into a ball. Tossing it carefully into the trash can, she added, "I'm going to miss my flight."

"Well, at least think about it while you're gone," Lorette implored, and she pulled the ball of paper from the can and carefully ironed it straight on the desktop. "It's not such a terrible idea."

"Lorette, please. I'm late. Say good-bye and wish me well."

"Good-bye and wish me well," she replied with the barest trace of a smile at the corner of her mouth. Then, with an exaggerated sigh, she lovingly folded the note and slipped it into the zippered pocket of Charlotte's bag. She gave it a couple of gentle pats for safekeeping. "And have a good time."

"In Vegas?" she returned. "Not likely. But I'll try."

A wedding in Las Vegas—she could never imagine something so unromantic! And yet, when she summoned up a picture of her friend Dyann, she couldn't imagine anything else. It was sure to be the most memorable wedding she'd ever witnessed, with the possible exception of Dyann's last one, which featured bungee-jumping off the side of a bridge in Key West.

She tucked away that promise ... *at least the weekend will be interesting!* ... and embarked on the endless trek through the Atlanta airport.

Charlotte never checked her bags when she traveled. It was too unpredictable. Her travel benefits afforded her the freedom of hopping a flight anywhere, even flying first class when it was available, for a meager $20 payroll deduction; however, it also meant traveling standby. And checking one's bags for a flight one might not actually make turned out to be far more hassle than it was worth.

It was part of the Global initiation process, and it seemed to happen only once before employees stepped predictably into the line of tradition, purchasing carry-ons and learning to pack so efficiently they could put even the staunchest military soldiers to shame.

"Charlotte Dennison," she stated as she set down the handwritten ticket and her Global identification on the counter at the gate.

"Are you in Reservations?" the woman behind the counter asked as she began to process the paperwork.

"Yes," Charlotte answered.

"I used to be. In Boston, before I finally got the airport job I'd been hoping for."

"I hear they're pretty hard to come by."

Charlotte wished the woman would just get on with it. A dozen passengers were in line behind her, and she didn't feel much like talking Global anyway.

"You know the drill," she finally said as she handed over the familiar blue envelope with the Global insignia across the front. "We'll call your name."

"Thanks."

Charlotte took a seat near the window and slid one leg sleekly over the other, leaning back into the chair with a sigh. Nothing to do now but wait. She had checked the load for her flight on the computer a couple of hours before leaving the office, and it looked fairly promising. She would surely make coach and, unless seven frequent flyers upgraded at the gate, she had a pretty good shot at first class.

She was excited to see Dyann again, although this would be the third wedding in ten years she had witnessed for her old friend. They'd known each other since grade school, and although Charlotte loved her, Dyann lived the exact kind of life she abhorred.

For one thing, there was no trace of a commitment to the "good Catholic girl" teachings they had both learned in parochial school. Then there was one failed relationship after another in Dyann's life, leaving behind a chain of broken promises to love completely, to stay forever, to work through any problem. Charlotte saw it over and over, with almost all of her friends, not just Dyann. And she resolved never to join the ranks of the deluded people who continued to make the same relationship mistakes again and again.

There were other things in life, after all—like travel. Since she'd come onboard at Global, she'd visited places she only used to dream about seeing. Luke's endless tales of Paris had inspired her, and her first trip as an airline employee was to the "City of Lights."

The French countryside was a sight she carried home with her and, if she could thank Paris for anything, it would be for lighting the spark of interest that caused her to utilize those travel benefits for everything they were worth.

In one year's time, she'd been to Athens, London, Lisbon, and Mexico, not to mention the countless American cities she and Lorette had toured on their days off. Trading days off were Charlotte's life's blood now.

Although she traveled considerably less the last couple of months, there were still so many places Charlotte wanted to experience. But even at $20 each way, or $40 internationally, travel still cost money. There were hotels and taxis and shuttles and, of course, food. Even though she'd cut her expenses to the barest bone to continue to travel, her paychecks still spread very thin when it came time to pay the bills each month. She managed, but it was still a struggle.

And then there was her father.

The thought of him shot a streak of acidic tension straight through her. He was the only family member she had left, and he didn't even know his daughter existed any more, much less what she was required to do to ensure his care and well-being.

She'd heard someone say on television once that Alzheimer's disease was a national tragedy—years before she experienced the truth of the statement firsthand, years before her mom had died, before Charlotte was left nothing but the shell of the man she'd idolized since childhood. He didn't even know her now, but Charlotte's love was large and bold just the same.

She slid her hand through her long chestnut hair and shut her hazel eyes.

"Oh, Daddy," she whispered, then ran both hands beneath the bangs that fell into her eyes. Tiredly, she rubbed both sides of her small upturned nose, fanning outward with her fingers to create a pinkish flush across the fair, faintly freckled skin of her china doll face.

How her father had nurtured her, she smiled to herself. And now it was her turn to nurture him. Standing in the large footprints of the example he had set, Charlotte vowed to never let him down. But the increased monthly bill at the nursing home threatened the fulfillment of that vow. She could hardly make ends meet as it was. How would she manage once the increase kicked in?

The finances won't be so scarce forever, she thought for the gazillionth time as a pot-bellied businessman plopped down in the chair beside her in the noisy airline terminal.

"We would now like to begin boarding Global Airlines flight number 2368, nonstop service to Las Vegas."

The woman behind the counter couldn't have been more than twenty-two, but her voice over the address system sounded older. She was obviously happy in her job, Charlotte thought. She'd found her niche.

"For those passengers holding first class tickets, or for passengers with small children or who might require a bit of extra assistance, please step up to gate number sixteen to begin our pre-boarding process."

Charlotte watched as a small swarm of travelers closed in around the doorway. A mother with two toddlers and an infant looked frazzled as she grappled with children's hands, a diaper bag, and the crying baby in her arms. Although the aura of family togetherness pinched slightly inside her chest, Charlotte silently hoped she wasn't seated anywhere near them once she boarded. She was looking forward to a peaceful flight.

Several businessmen quickly presented tickets to the attendant and moved on past. One of them, a nice-looking man in a charcoal gray suit, stood out to Charlotte. Not because of his looks, although he was quite appealing. His sandy hair was silken and reflected wisps of light that were almost gold, and Charlotte noticed his eyes were a striking blue as he combed the hair from his face with long, manicured fingers.

Very cute, she thought before looking back at what had caught her attention to begin with: his scuffed shoes.

Someone ought to tutor that boy in the art of professional appearance. Probably new to the business world.

The rest of the passengers lined up at the boarding call, looking like cattle behind the pasture fence. Charlotte made a mental count of four other passengers, probably Global employees or members of their families, also waiting for their names to be called. Flying standby was such a long process, sometimes resulting in a mad rush to the pay-phones to call the Global Airlines 800 number and find out the next appropriate flight.

If she didn't make this flight, there was one to Los Angeles in a little while, she recalled. Perhaps she could rent a car and drive across the desert to Vegas from there.

It was a relief when the woman went back to the counter and began to print out more boarding passes. This meant the standbys had probably made it onto the flight.

"Taylor. Biscayne. Dennison. And Matovich."

A familiar surge of relief mixed with excitement made its way through every vein in Charlotte's body.

"First class," the woman said as she handed Charlotte a pass. "Seat 3-C."

She'd been hoping for a window seat, but she wasn't going to quibble. She got on! Perhaps she'd call Dyann from the plane and tell her the good news, she thought, but then dismissed the idea as a frivolous expense.

After stowing her overnight bag in the compartment above the seat, Charlotte settled down into 3-C with her purse and the black leather bag beside her. She loved the leg room in first class. Even as trim as she was, coach seats hardly afforded any personal space. She found herself wondering what they would serve for a late-night snack as she snapped the buckle on her seatbelt and adjusted the strap.

She realized when she caught a quick glimpse of his shoes that she hadn't even noticed 3-A. *Mr. Scuff-Shoe,* she thought, then gave him a polite smile.

"Hi," he returned, then after a moment added, "Seth Pruitt."

Oh no, she sighed to herself. *A talker.*

"Charlotte Dennison."

A stiff nod, and then she looked away.

They usually get the message from that, she thought.

She didn't usually indulge, but Charlotte accepted a chilled crystal glass of champagne from the flight attendant. It was a special occasion, after all. It wasn't every day that she flew across the country to witness the wedding of her oldest friend. *Every other year. But not every day.*

"To a quick and easy flight," Seth Pruitt said as he offered his glass of orange juice toward her in a toast, and she politely clinked her glass against it. She liked the crystal-clear tone of his voice in contrast to her more smoky pitch.

"And no turbulence," she added.

His chuckle drew her gaze, and she noticed that his smile seemed to emblazon his entire face. And, to be honest, that light had spread across the seat and touched her, diffusing all the way down into the pit of her stomach.

Scuffy shoes and all, there was something very appealing about 3-A. The spicy scent of him drifted around her in a gentle cloud, and she watched him down the last drop of juice from the glass before handing it back to the flight attendant. Charlotte noted that the woman was the fortunate recipient of one of his smiles, and she found herself somewhat envious before she had time to capture and control the emotion.

Stop it, she warned herself as the plane left the runway. *Just stop it right now.*

She made a mental promise not to breathe a word about the handsome gentleman seated beside her on the plane within Lorette's mighty earshot.

"You passed up someone fabulous?" she could just hear her say.

"Not everyone finds a husband like James," she'd told her friend a thousand times or so. "Not everyone finds someone fabulous."

As the landing gear lifted into the belly of the plane, Charlotte heaved a deep, labored sigh.

Not everyone is even looking for someone fabulous, she thought.

But if I were, Seth Pruitt might be one candidate well worth considering.

Chapter Two

Charlotte despised take-off, but once in the air she usually managed to relax a bit. She wondered if the fluttering of butterflies that persisted well after the seat belt sign had been turned off was due to lingering anxiety, hunger, or just the occupant of seat 3-A.

"Would you like the window seat?" he asked.

He must have noticed how she was straining to look out at the lights below.

"Oh, no," she replied. "I was just looking for a moment. It helps me get my balance."

"Don't fly much?"

"Actually, yes," she said with a smile. "I fly quite a bit. I just can't seem to learn to enjoy it."

"It's more natural to me these days than starting up my car," said Seth, leaning back into his seat. "I've seen twelve cities this month alone. Sometimes I wake up in the morning and have to check my planner to see where I am."

"Let me guess," she teased. "A rock star on a world tour?"

"With a daily planner?" he asked, giving her one of those smiles that set her heart to pounding. "Freelance architect striking out on my own."

"An architect! How exciting."

"It will be, I think. Once I build up my business. Right now I'm spending more money per month on airfare than I have to spend on any three utility bills."

"Assuming you're ever home long enough to run up the utilities," she pointed out.

"Exactly," he agreed. "What about you? What line are you in?"

"Reservations," she replied, turning in her seat slightly to face him, slipping one leg casually over the other. "I probably booked you on this flight."

"You work for Global?"

"Yes. For over a year now."

"And how do you like it?"

"Well, I like the travel benefits, that's for sure!" She chuckled. Then, more seriously, she added, "I like the job, too."

"I've probably paid your salary on what I've poured into Global."

"I'd been wondering where to send the thank-you note," she replied, and he stared at her for a long moment. His gaze was warm and she felt heated color rise up like steam into her face.

"Would either of you like a light snack?" the attendant asked, and it was almost painful to Charlotte to re-focus her attention on anything besides Seth.

"What is it?" he asked, then lifted his eyebrows in a questioning manner, waiting to hear something he liked.

"A cold platter," she explained, and Charlotte didn't like the way the attendant's eyes locked onto Seth's as she continued. "Mesquite breast of chicken with red potato salad and a fresh fruit bowl."

"Sounds good," he said. "I'll have some."

"Me, too," Charlotte added—as if the attendant had even noticed her sitting there.

"And to drink?" the woman cooed at Seth.

"An iced tea would go nicely with that, don't you think?"

Charlotte waited for a standard girlish acknowledgment from the woman. When it didn't come, she realized Seth had been talking to her.

"Oh, yes it does," she agreed, and wondered if she sounded as southern-belle to him as she had to herself.

"Two iced teas then."

"Coming right up." She looked to Charlotte like a cat who was about to pounce on a nice, fat parakeet. "My name is Grace. If you need anything at all."

"Why do I have the feeling she doesn't mean me?" Charlotte muttered as she watched Grace make her way down the aisle. Was there a dramatic increase to the sway factor of her gait, or was Charlotte just imagining things?

"Pardon?"

"Oh, nothing. . . . So where do you live?"

"New York," he replied as he pulled the black leather portfolio from beside his seat and laid it flat on his lap.

"You don't strike me as your typical New Yorker," Charlotte said, grinning.

"Excellent perception."

He returned her smile as he glanced over several pages of loose paperwork, then tucked them neatly into the fold inside the case.

"I'm originally from Lexington, Kentucky."

"The Bluegrass State," she said. "We're practically neighbors."

"You're from Atlanta then?"

"Roswell. Born and bred."

"My family raised racehorses," he told her. "An aspiring architect didn't exactly fit into the scheme of things out on the ranch."

"I see your dilemma. But New York?"

"I studied there," he continued. "Then stayed to make my fortune."

"Which you haven't quite made yet."

"Precisely. And at this rate, I'm beginning to wonder if I ever will. You don't like New York?"

"No," she said. "Sorry. Everyone seems to work so hard to get anywhere there. No one drives cars. They just take this bus to that train, then transfer to the other train. By the time you get where you're going, you could have been there and done your business back in Atlanta!"

"So what's your hurry?" he asked. "And they say New Yorkers are in a constant state of rush."

Their conversation moved on in a smooth sort of motion, with no silent gaps, no uncomfortable lulls, and Charlotte noted that there was something quite paradoxical about Seth Pruitt. He was boyish in the open way he talked about himself. She knew more about him in the hour they'd left the ground than she did about many people she had known much longer.

His humor was candid and warm, and those scuffed shoes of his had actually grown on her since she first saw them back in the Atlanta airport. And yet there were moments of sheer machismo, the way he would look at her or react to something she'd said, so masculine and powerful that she felt like she might explode beneath its weight.

Charlotte checked to make sure his attention was focused

on the contents of the case in front of him, then took a long hard look at him. The lines of his face didn't even show until he smiled, and the blue of his eyes seemed to outshine the backdrop of the heavens through the window behind him. His mouth was just about the most kissable she had ever seen up close, and she found herself preoccupied with silly imaginings of leaning over . . . and . . .

"Your food."

She jumped when he said it, and she guiltily tore her gaze from him like a bandage from a scraped knee—quick, clean, and painful.

"Thank you," she said hoarsely to Grace, who only hummed a polite response as she leaned across her to place Seth's meal carefully down on his tray table. "Can I get you anything else?"

"No. Thanks though."

He seemed utterly oblivious to her blatant flirtation, which made him even more appealing to Charlotte. He wasn't one of those men who expected every woman to ogle his every move, nor even reacted to it when they inevitably did. But he had to notice it, she decided. He must have chosen to ignore it.

Charlotte wanted to stop herself from hanging on his every word. She reminded herself again and again during the flight that she had no interest in romance. She knew she was taking on the schoolgirl quality she despised so much in other women. But she couldn't stop herself!

Her hormones were suddenly raging, and she felt as if everyone else on the flight could see it. Even Seth, but she knew he'd be too polite to point it out, the same way he pretended not to notice Grace as she salivated over him like a panther over its prey.

Don't listen so intently, she warned herself as he told her his hopes for future projects and showed her the plans for the highrise office building he'd been pitching in Atlanta. *Don't lean in so close*, she thought. *And, for heaven's sake, stop taking in the scent of him as if your life depended on it.*

She hated the idle conversation of fellow travelers. Normally, she went out of her way to avoid hearing their life stories. At times, she had even feigned sleep to put an end to their ceaseless babble.

What is so different this time? she wondered. She'd sat beside attractive men on other flights. The man she'd met on the flight to Athens looked like a Greek sculpture come to life. He romanced her relentlessly all the way over to his native country. She just wasn't interested. And he'd been far more attractive than Seth Pruitt!

What is wrong with you? she asked herself. *Have you lost your mind?*

She finally decided the only way to gain a bit of perspective was to step away from the situation.

"Excuse me," she muttered as she snapped the buckle of the seatbelt and slipped from her seat, fumbling with the leather bag at her side and lifting the small brown purse from beneath it.

"Oh, Seth," she mouthed sarcastically at herself in the bathroom mirror a moment later, and she fluttered her eyelashes dramatically. "You're *sooooo* right. An iced tea goes divinely with cold chicken."

The two had complemented each other perfectly, but Charlotte didn't feel like admitting that right then.

"Bleh!" she groaned, poking her tongue out at her reflection in the mirror. "You're ridiculous! And you're behaving like a lovesick child. Get a . . . grip!!"

Another artist was getting her insides racing like a locomotive. It was Luke all over again.

It may have taken a good ten minutes but, by the time

Charlotte flicked open the "occupied" lever on the lavatory door, she had talked herself right back into line. Seth Pruitt was just another man on the flight to Las Vegas, no more interesting than anyone else; no more attractive than any other businessman in first class. He was just one of the masses. One more valued passenger for Global Airlines.

"Did you leave this on the seat for me, or is placing this ad just another thing on your 'to do' list?"

Charlotte wasn't sure if it was turbulence that knocked her off her feet into 3-C or if it was the sight of Seth holding that crumpled piece of paper she thought she'd thrown away.

Lorette!

How had it fallen out? Had he been rifling through her things while she was gone? What kind of man was this Seth Pruitt?

" 'Wanted . . . Single white male professional with an eye for a bargain,' " he read, then glanced up at her beneath arched eyebrows. "Did you leave it on the seat in hopes that I'd save you the price of the classified?"

"I did not leave it on my seat!" she stammered, flicking the paper from his hand with a loud snap. "It was a joke. A . . . bad joke. My friend Lorette . . ."

"Please, Charlotte," he said as he leaned in toward her. "We don't have to play games here. What exactly did you have in mind?"

He was enjoying the moment, and she worked hard to suppress the urge to strangle him with her bare hands.

"Is this an invitation of some kind?" he asked her coyly, then quickly snatched up her entire arm by the wrist and the paper from her grip. " 'Must love to travel and enjoy being single,' " he read, holding her off easily with one hand. " 'Want to experience everything this world has to offer? Then this is the ad to answer.' "

Charlotte succeeded in taking the paper from him when he was through, and only because he allowed her to take it, which enraged her even more. To make matters worse, their fellow travelers noticed their scuffle and, as a Global employee, Charlotte was keenly aware that she was to be as discreet a passenger as possible. This was hardly discreet behavior!

She crunched up the paper in her fist, then turned straight in her seat and focused on the back of the chair in front of her.

"This is a dangerous world, Charlotte," Seth said, breaking the silence a moment later. "An ad like this could get a girl into seriously hot water."

"That's Ms. Dennison to you, thank you very much," she seethed without looking at him. "And I'm not a girl," she added. "I'm a woman."

"But no lady, is that it?"

Charlotte snapped her head around to look at him, so abruptly she strained her neck. "How dare you!"

"It wasn't an observation," he responded. "Just an inquiry."

"How about this, Mr. Pruitt. Keep your inquires to yourself for the next forty minutes or so. Then we'll land in Las Vegas and go our separate ways. I'm going to make every effort to forget I met you at all. Why don't you do the same?"

"On the contrary, Ms. *Den-ni-son*," he enunciated. "I won't be forgetting you for quite a long while."

Several moments passed before she felt any type of movement at all from his seat, and out of the corner of her eye she noted that he had returned his attention to the portfolio he carried with him.

"Can I take your empty glass?" Grace cooed at him just before the captain turned on the "Fasten Seat Belt" sign, and he flashed her one his despicable grins. Charlotte could feel its heat without even seeing it.

"Thank you for flying Global." She smiled back.

"Grace," he said with a sigh. "It was my pleasure."

Oh brother! thought Charlotte. And she couldn't believe, even for a moment, that he was any different from every other man in the world. Not notice that women were swooning in his path? This guy was eating it up like manna off streets of gold!

Charlotte stood up the moment the aircraft came to a stop and tugged her bag down from the overhead compartment. As she turned, Seth moved past her without so much as a nod.

So why would she expect a cad like him to have any manners anyway?

"Welcome to Las Vegas," the flight attendants chanted as weary travelers moved past them off the plane. "Thank you for flying Global."

Charlotte resisted the urge to buck him right in the fanny with her overnight bag when Seth stopped in front of her and lingered over Grace's handshake.

"Enjoy your time in Las Vegas," she told him sweetly. "Some of the crew is taking an extra day over at Bally's if you find yourself with some time on your hands."

"I'll keep that in mind, Grace," he replied as he took the folded slip of paper she handed him. Charlotte looked away and bit her tongue. She desperately wanted to give him a hearty shove right off that airplane!

Charlotte kept her distance as they moved through the Las Vegas airport, then heaved a sigh of relief when his profile turned toward baggage claim as she went out the terminal door.

Las Vegas was hot even at midnight, and Charlotte recalled how much she despised the arid desert climate. She remembered that the desert was hot in the daytime and cold at night. Seth Pruitt's presence seemed to throw off everything—even the forces of nature!

"Can you take me to The Excalibur?" she asked softly as she climbed into the back of the nearest taxi.

"You got it," the jovial man replied, and he hit the gas the moment she slammed the door shut.

She fought the urge to strain a look into baggage claim as they sped past, and tensely clasped her hands in her lap. It was only then that she realized she was still clutching the wad of paper with Lorette's handwriting scribbled across it.

She thought she saw him out of the corner of her eye, but she refused to look.

"In town on business or pleasure?" the cabbie inquired idly.

"Torture," she replied as she let the paper loose out the window into the night, and there was no further conversation between the airport and the hotel.

Chapter Three

Charlotte had intended to take a cool shower immediately after checking into her room at The Excalibur, but she was far too tired once she actually arrived. The king-sized bed was inviting, and her weary body craved sleep. She didn't even bother to dig her nightshirt out of her bag. She just stripped down to nothing and crawled in.

When Dyann pounded on her door the next morning, it took Charlotte several minutes to wake up. She was still groggy when she stumbled to the door wrapped in the bed-sheet, her hair mussed and hanging straight into her face.

"You look like crud!" her friend cried as she pulled her into an embrace. "But I don't care. I can't believe you're here!"

"Dyann, come inside, for heaven's sake. I'm not even dressed."

"No, wait, I want you to meet Billy," she protested, fling-

23

ing the door wide open despite Charlotte's attempts to shut it.

"No, Dy, not now. Let me get a shower and put on some makeup. I didn't get checked in and into bed until after two, and . . ."

"Billy, come in here. This is my Char!"

"Oh, dear." Charlotte was shell-shocked. The morning was moving far too quickly for her. "Dy, please."

"And this is Billy's best man, Seth Pruitt."

Charlotte stopped breathing momentarily as she adjusted to the sudden tilt of the floor. Her fingers got tangled in the mess of hair she tried to force away from her face as she struggled with her bedsheet. She said a silent prayer that it wasn't open somewhere she didn't know about.

"You?" she mumbled.

"*Ms. Dennison* is your maid of honor?"

"You two know each other?" Dyann asked. "Why didn't you tell me you knew each other?"

"We sat next to each other on the flight out from Atlanta," he explained, then looked down at the floor.

"Atlanta, that's right!" Dyann tittered. "You both flew in from Atlanta!"

Charlotte glared at Dyann.

"Why don't we all get out of here, Dy," Billy suggested, "and let this little lady get dressed. It's obvious this is a bad time."

"Yes," Charlotte agreed. She heard Seth sigh, but she couldn't bring herself to look directly at him.

"Okay, you boys go on down to the buffet." Dyann gave them a shove. "We'll meet you down there once Char is ready to face the living."

Seth made the first exit, and she was more than mildly relieved. Billy lingered in the doorway with Dyann, and just when she thought she might have to vacate the room to give them some privacy, they managed to come apart.

"Nice meeting you," Billy said, a chuckle escaping, then Dyann closed the door behind him.

Charlotte made her way across the spinning room and collapsed on the bed, smothering her face with the pillow.

"Oh, Char! . . . You met on the plane? Did you get a look at that poor, pathetic girl who left the note on the seat for Seth?"

Charlotte yanked the pillow from her face and flung it across the room at her friend. "It's so nice to see you again after all these months, Dy. Why don't you just pull out a club and beat me with it now and get it over with, huh?"

"Char . . . you're not that girl . . . are you?"

"I don't know what that overblown egomaniac told you, but that's not the way it happened!"

"Oh, no, you are?" Dyann raced across the room and bounced down on the bed beside her. "Char, no. A personal ad?"

"Would you stop it? My friend from work, Lorette, had this crazy idea. It was a joke mostly. I said I'd never get married . . . you know how I always said I'd never get married again . . . and she said it was a shame to waste those spouse benefits. She . . . she came up with this ridiculous scheme. She wrote it out and put it in my bag. It fell out when I pulled out my purse and went to the bathroom. . . . Oh, forget it, just forget it! I can't believe he told you about it!"

"Oh, yeah." She tried not to laugh. "We all went over to Bally's after he got in last night and . . ."

"Bally's?"

Charlotte's blood rose to an instant boil as she struggled to shake away the image of Grace handing Seth that slip of paper as he left the plane.

"I just want to go home."

"Home?" she cried. "You can't. Did you forget why you came? My wedding?!"

"Oh, Dy, please. Under these circumstances . . ."

"What circumstances?" she argued. "So you and Seth got off on the wrong foot. It's not like you're the ones getting married! It's me and Billy, and we want our two dearest friends in the whole wide world to stand beside us. Well, actually . . . sit . . . behind us. We've rented this amazing pink convertible Cadillac, and we're going over to this drive-thru chapel . . ."

"You've got to be kidding."

"No. It's going to be so cool."

"How old are you, Dy? I thought growing up that we were the same age, but how old are you really? Did you leave a decade or so behind when I wasn't looking?"

"I'm twenty-eight, just like you," she said as she placed an arm around Charlotte's shoulder. "And I enjoy my life!"

"To the fullest extent of the law," Charlotte mumbled.

"I would think you'd like a little of that to rub off on you."

Charlotte couldn't help but laugh. Maybe Dyann was right. Maybe she should loosen up a little.

"A drive-thru wedding chapel," she muttered, then shook her head and fell against her friend in a fit of laughter. "Only you, Dy. Only you."

Seth followed Bill straight to the beverage bar and poured himself a cup of coffee. The French toast on a passing plate drew his attention, but he decided to wait a polite and respectable amount of time for the women to join them.

One cup. Fifteen minutes. Not one minute longer, he thought.

"Over here?" Bill pointed out a booth, and Seth nodded in agreement.

Charlotte Dennison.

She was a strange one, Charlotte. And yet there was a disconcerting vulnerability about her that had driven him insane since meeting her on the plane. He could close his eyes, even now, and see that mane of shining hair, taste that floral scent that was her.

What was it about her? he wondered. Even at her angriest, she had reeled him in like an expert fisherman. For the duration of the flight, he'd been as hooked as a bass.

"So what's the story on Dyann's friend, Charlotte?" he asked, trying to appear casual as he paused to take a long sip from his mug.

"Tell the truth, buddy," Bill asked. "Is she the one you met on the plane?"

The expectant grin on his face was contagious.

"She's the one," he returned with a chuckle.

"All the stories Dy has told me about her, that's the one thing I'd never have guessed. She's advertising for a husband!"

Seth fought off the sudden urge to defend her. What other explanation could there possibly be? He recalled how devastated she appeared when he held the note up to her. Maybe it really was a joke. Or maybe her devastation was because he had flatly rejected her.

"Okay," he said as he leaned in toward Bill. "I want to know everything you've got on Charlotte Dennison. And don't leave anything out."

Dyann talked nonstop through Charlotte's shower and over the hum of her blow dryer. It was almost a relief when she grew weary or bored of watching Charlotte get ready and decided to look for Seth and Bill.

"I'll meet you downstairs later then," she called through the bathroom door. "Why don't you order yourself some coffee to wake up?"

That struck Charlotte as a wonderful idea. Breakfast in her room rather than gathering around the buffet with a couple of dozen hungry gamblers—and Seth.

She asked herself a hundred times how this mess could have happened while she applied her makeup and picked at the breakfast that was delivered. The sheer horrible co-incidence of it!

She could already hear Lorette telling her that there is no such thing as coincidence, that everything on the planet happens for a reason, that there is a purpose for every speck of activity. Charlotte desperately wanted to tell her to hush, and Lorette wasn't even in the state!

Suddenly, there was a slight rap on the door. She stared for a moment making no move to answer it.

"Come on, Ms. Dennison. Open up. I know you're in there," Seth said.

Her heart started beating wildly and without any discernible rhythm.

"Would you please stop calling me Ms. Dennison?" she asked as she yanked the door open, leaving him standing in the doorway.

"Did I hear wrong? Isn't that what you asked me to call you?"

"Shut up."

It isn't Lorette, but he'll do.

"Look," he began, and Charlotte sat down on the wing-back chair at the edge of the sitting area. "I know this is awkward, but this weekend isn't about us. It's about Bill and Dyann. Can't we put our own feelings aside and do this for them? Can't we both be big enough to do that?"

"Don't talk to me about big!" she shouted. Then she

leaned back and regrouped, taking a deep breath. "I'm big enough," she said, calmer. "Are you big enough?"

"I think so," he said. "So we'll both try then?"

"Yes."

"Truce?"

Charlotte looked up to find him standing over her, his hand extended. It was one long moment before she accepted the peace offering.

"Can you believe two grown people getting married at a drive-thru wedding chapel?" he asked her finally, and she couldn't help but chuckle.

"Now that we're going to speak to each other again," she said, "would you like a cup of coffee? When I ordered a pot, they brought me three cups."

"Thanks, I would, but only if you'll explain something to me."

"The note?" she groaned.

"Of course! What was that?"

Charlotte drew a ragged breath as she poured two cups from the plastic pitcher. "Cream?"

"Please."

"I have this *ex-friend* named Lorette," she said, then paused with a grin. "She's happily married to James the Magnificent. She has the life she's always dreamed of having. No worries. And she thinks everyone else on the planet should have the opportunity to be as *faaaabulously* happy as she is."

"The witch."

"Right. Well, we were having this discussion one day about the salary at Global and how a single woman can hardly afford to live on it. I had told her before that I would never get married again and—"

"Again? You're divorced?"

"Yes. And I don't ever want to do it again."

"Don't you think you're being a little narrow-minded?"

"Are you going to let me tell this story or not?"

"Please," he replied. "The floor is all yours."

"So Lorette gets this idea. I don't want to be married, but I have these incredible travel benefits that are free to a spouse. She says maybe there's some guy out there who has some extra money who wants or needs to travel. A sick sister in Tel Aviv or something, and he has to go over every month."

"Or an aspiring rock star with the chance for a world tour?"

Despite his crooked grin, she glared at him. "I thought the floor was mine, Pruitt."

"Sorry. Continue, please."

"So this guy, whoever he is out there, might be spending a fortune on travel for whatever reason. So maybe he would be saving a lot of money if he paid me, say, seven hundred and fifty dollars every month in return for unlimited travel on Global. Well, Lorette says a thousand dollars."

"Yeah, I wouldn't settle for less than a thousand dollars myself. It's a big step to . . ."

"Pruitt."

"Sorry."

"So she writes up this personal ad, puts it on my desk, and it ends up in my bag."

"Until it falls out and I find it."

"Exactly."

"So you weren't leaving me some sort of invitation."

"Of course not," she replied. "What kind of woman do you think I am?"

"Certainly not the kind who would be stupid enough to place an ad like that for any degenerate to answer, that's for sure."

"Whether you believe me or not, Seth," she told him softly, "I never had any intention of placing that ad."

"I do believe you."

He seemed to be able to recognize the weariness in her eyes, and he raised up from his chair and stood over her for a moment.

"You're a beautiful woman, Charlotte," he said, so quietly that she almost didn't hear it. "Don't sell yourself short."

"Oh, it's not that, I don't think," she said, curling up in the chair with her cup of coffee, as he sat on the arm of the chair beside her. "It's not that I can't find a man. I just don't want to. The whole dumb conversation arose from the realization that money is a necessity of life, and I'm not making enough of it. I can't travel the way I want to. And I have my dad in a nursing home."

"Yes." He nodded. "Alzheimer's. Bill was telling me. It must be very difficult for you."

His sincere concern touched her for a moment, catching her off guard. She absorbed the feeling for a moment before continuing.

"And then there's the fact that I live in the back part of someone else's house, and I'd love to have a home of my own," she continued. "Except that I'm trying to save every cent I can afford to take these trips I'm entitled to. I want to see the world, you know? I've wanted to ever since I was a little girl. And now the whole world is opened up to me, and I can't afford to run through the door!"

"I understand the frustration." He nodded, pouring himself another half-cup from the Thermos and sitting down across from her. "I'm averaging twenty-five hundred every month on airfare alone. Even when I do make some real money on a project, it all goes back into Global Airlines, or TWA, or Delta, or whoever offers the best rate for the next trip I have to take."

"Striking out on your own can't be easy," she commented. "Or cheap."

"No." He managed a weak chuckle. "It's neither one of those."

Charlotte smiled warmly at him just then. She couldn't help herself. He was so easy to be with, to talk to. She trusted him with her feelings, and she could see that he trusted her too. It was a cozy scene, the two of them sitting there, sipping coffee and sharing their dreams. She could hardly believe not even twenty-four hours had passed since they first met.

"I have a three-year plan," he told her, and she eagerly sat up. "For the next two years, I'll drum up as much work as I can. Individual projects, city planning, industrial parks, condo developments, whatever I can manage. Then, by my thirty-second birthday, I want to begin building my own complexes and putting them up for resale. I figure the people I've worked for during the last year and over the next two, the people with the real money, will back me up because they'll have already seen what I can do."

Charlotte was sorry when he stopped. She was enjoying the opportunity to share a piece of his vision.

"I'm sorry," he said as he shook his head at himself. "I get on this subject and just go off. I don't always realize not everyone is as engrossed in this whole thing as I am. Dyann keeps asking me why I'm not involved with anyone. You've just seen firsthand the reason why."

"I know exactly what you mean," she told him. "I have sort of a three-year plan, too, although I never really looked at it in any sort of timeframe. I figured I'd use this time to provide the care my dad needs. I can travel and see all the places I've always dreamed of seeing. I've been to Buck-

ingham Palace, and to Crete, and I've ridden a hot air balloon in Africa! But there are lots of dreams left."

"Such as?"

"Well . . ."

She grinned, almost embarrassed.

"I have this dream of sitting in a gondola in Venice,
barefoot, while some lovely Italian man rows me through
the canals."

"I've heard it smells really bad there."

"This is my fantasy, Pruitt. Leave it alone."

"Sorry."

"And however long it takes . . ."

Grief rose up into the back of her throat suddenly, sur-
prising her. She pushed the wave of emotion back down
into place.

"However long he has left . . . my dad . . . I'll make him
as happy and as comfortable as I can."

Seth reached over and gave her hand a quick squeeze.

"I'll have put in my time in Reservations and learned as
much about the company as I possibly can in the meantime.
Then I'll stop the day trades and the travel, other than my
regular vacation each year, and I'll begin my rise to the
top."

"CEO of Global Airlines?"

"Maybe."

"These are big dreams we have, Ms. Dennison."

"Yes, they are," she said softly, and they shared a smile
that warmed her. There was a comfortableness between
them that might have alarmed her had she been able to
break free of it long enough to stand back and really look
at it.

A ray of sunlight beamed through the window and cast
glimmering streaks of gold through Seth's hair. For the first
time, she realized how thoroughly he filled out the pair of

faded jeans he was wearing. He did not have a bulky, body-builder physique, but his muscular lines shone through the white cotton shirt which was set off by a pair of navy pin-striped suspenders. His sleeves were rolled to the elbows, and she noticed that his hands were strong and aged beyond his years.

He must work with his hands a lot, she concluded.

The boots that poked out from beneath his 501s were as scuffed as the loafers he'd been wearing on the plane, and Charlotte grinned at the memory.

He's a beautiful man, this Mr. Scuff-Shoe, she thought. *Really beautiful.*

"Tell me I'm crazy," he started to say, and the broken silence seemed to slither slowly up into her soul.

"What?"

She looked at him, and he seemed like someone else at that moment. Seth, but someone else, too.

"What is it?" she asked again.

"Charlotte?"

She loved the sound of her name when it floated from his lips. She waited, but he had stopped.

"Charlotte?"

"Pruitt?"

"Keep an open mind."

"What is it?"

"Ms. Dennison . . . will you . . . marry me?"

Chapter Four

Charlotte roared with laughter. But Seth didn't.

"Marry you?" she exclaimed. "Very funny, Pruitt."

"I'm not joking."

"Are you out of your mind?"

"Maybe," he began, then moved to the edge of his chair, pausing for a moment. *Perhaps he had lost his mind completely*, he thought. "I can afford to pay you a thousand dollars per month, Charlotte. That would cover your father's extra expenses, wouldn't it?"

"I . . . uh . . . guess so . . ."

She couldn't think straight.

"You go to Venice and ride through the stinky canals, and start saving for that house you want. In the meantime, I'm saving over a grand every month on travel. At least! Money I can put back into my business."

"You're kidding."

"Maybe your friend Lorette is not as psychotic as we

first thought," he suggested, wondering if indeed he was the psychotic one. "Maybe this could work for us both."

"Or maybe Lorette is as psychotic as I thought, and you're even worse." Was she reading his mind? "I could lose my job, Seth."

"No one at Global would ever have to know," he suggested, and he was amazed at his conviction despite the wrenches of doubt clouding his soul. "As far as they would know, I'm exactly who you know me to be. An architect who travels all the time. You said yourself that the place you're in is too small. You can move into a bigger place and they'll assume it's so that there's room for the both of us."

Am I actually making sense of this idea? he wondered, grinning to himself. *Am I nuts?*

The responses dancing in Charlotte's head turned her hazel eyes to a vivid emerald green, and Seth watched as she considered the points he was presenting. It probably seemed as far-fetched to her as it did to him when the word crept up from the pit of his soul and had the audacity to pass over his lips: Marriage.

Marriage was a daunting concept. He hadn't allowed himself to even utter the word for a very long time—not since Michele.

His reason not to marry had begun to take on a life of its own and here it was now, alive and standing tall before them. And to his surprise and amazement, it seemed almost conceivable

They would both benefit from the arrangement; no one would lose. He'd been praying for a solution to his travel problems. And there were no accidents in this life, after all. Seth was sure of that.

"Pruitt," she repeated for the second or third time, and again nothing followed.

"We have a great deal to offer one another," he told her, and she looked at him wordlessly, her full red lips parted slightly.

The only hard part would be keeping things platonic, he realized as her beauty settled in on him.

It would have to be a business arrangement alone, and nothing more. Cash for her, travel for him. Period. A platonic arrangement.

He repeated the word platonic in his mind again as an extra reminder.

The distance between them would take care of that, he assured himself. This could work! This crazy idea that started out as a joke was actually a feasible solution to financial problems they'd both been battling.

He wondered what she was thinking. There was something suddenly there, some kind of fire dancing in her eyes that hadn't been there before. Had she come to a decision? Was she going to *agree?*

Charlotte erased the mental images slowly and deliberately that had suddenly crept up on her. Sunday mornings with Seth as her husband, reading the *New York Times,* sipping hot tea in the sunlight, his hair glistening in much the same way it was just then. She chastised herself for the fantasy. That was not the picture he'd been painting, nor was it the offer he was making.

"We wouldn't have to change our lives in the least," he continued. "Not in any sacrificial way, anyhow."

Despite the itch at the base of her spine she couldn't quite reach, the proposal was eerily beginning to make sense. She forced the nagging doubt from her mind and looked at the whole and complete picture, as if Seth had raised one of his blueprints for her inspection. It wasn't as if she hoped for any sincere considerations of marriage—

from Seth or anyone else! She didn't want to fall in love. She didn't want a husband in her everyday routine.

So, why couldn't this work? she thought.

"It would afford us both such a huge degree of freedom, Charlotte. We'd have to keep in touch on, say, a monthly basis," he suggested. "So you would know enough about what's going on with me that you could talk intelligently about it if you were asked."

"Because you'd eventually run into someone from Global who knew me on one of those flights," she added. "There could be no romances with flight attendants."

"Romances with . . ."

He paused, and then her meaning was suddenly clear. "Oh. Well. I wouldn't exactly call Grace a romance, Ms. Dennison."

"If you're going to pick up strange women, Pruitt, they cannot be employed by Global Airlines," she stated firmly. "Agreed?"

"Agreed."

And she thought she noticed a slight quiver at the corner of his mouth before he turned away.

"So what do you say to a double drive-thru wedding?" he asked finally.

"In the pink Cadillac?" she asked, laughing.

"Bill and Dyann would love it," he said. "And I don't suppose it much matters where we do it since it's not really going to be . . . you know."

There stood the hair at the back of her neck again.

"Right. But we'll need rings. Real ones."

"We'll go out this afternoon and look for something tasteful, but reasonable."

"You mean cheap," she said with a grin.

"Precisely."

Charlotte couldn't believe things were happening so fast.

She was on a cartoon rocketship spinning out of control. This was so unlike her, and she had the feeling it was unlike Seth, too, although she wasn't acquainted with him well enough to know for sure.

"Are we really going to do this?" she asked him after several minutes of silence.

"I'm willing if you are."

"I think so."

"I need you to know so. We both need you to know so."

And Charlotte knew he was right.

The day was unusually overcast, and Charlotte wondered if it was going to rain. It would figure. A planned wedding in the back of a convertible was almost an engraved invitation for a thunderstorm.

She couldn't help but wonder if she didn't deserve it. Maybe what they were doing was like laughing at the sanctity of marriage, using it for their own specific purposes, and the rain was their punishment.

"But isn't that ultimately what everyone does?" Dyann asked her that afternoon as the two of them moved ahead of Bill and Seth on the crowded main strip. "Everyone marries for their own inner reasons. No one walks into it without some sort of an agenda."

"That could be the most unromantic thing I've ever heard in my life," Charlotte replied sadly. "Especially from a woman who's getting married tonight for real."

"But this isn't about romance with you and Seth, is it?"

That question raised a painful doubt inside Charlotte. At least with Luke, no matter what the outcome, she had married for love. At least there was some degree of affection there, an actual intention—no matter how misguided!—to stay together, to build a life together.

None of the rings they saw in three jewelry stores appealed to Charlotte. The ring was going to be more a part of her daily life than the husband! She should at least have one she liked.

"What about here?" Dyann asked as they came upon a pawn shop with an antique wedding dress in the front window.

She and Seth exchanged casual shrugs, and the foursome filed inside.

"Can I help you?" the elderly man asked from behind the counter.

"They're looking for a wedding ring," Dyann told him, looping her arm through Bill's and pulling him close to her.

"I have some beauties here," he offered, and Charlotte and Seth stepped up the display while Dyann led Bill toward the racks of vintage clothes.

The two of them glanced over several rows of velvet cases holding diamond solitaires, wedding sets, and bands. A delicate circle of small diamonds caught Charlotte's eye.

"This one's lovely."

The old man didn't miss a beat and produced the band, placing it in Charlotte's palm.

"Try it on," Seth said, leaning in for a closer look.

Charlotte turned the ring over in her hand several times. There was engraving on the inside, and she held it up to the light to take a closer look.

"Here's to twenty-five more years," she read, then looked sadly into Seth's eyes. "That's so tragic. After twenty-five years of marriage, this ends up in a pawn shop."

"You kids can turn the story around," the broker said. "Give that ring a new happy home."

Charlotte slipped the ring onto her finger. A perfect fit.

"I think it goes on the left hand," Seth told her.

"It's bad luck to try a wedding ring on the ring finger

before the ceremony," she instinctively replied. Then the two of them exchanged a smile.

"It's only two hundred." The old guy wanted a sale. "Well worth seven-fifty."

"They're not going to pay a penny more than a hundred," Bill called, and the broker studied Seth.

"One hundred." Seth nodded. "It's all I can afford."

"One-fifty, and I'll throw in a plain gold band for the groom," he tested.

"Sold."

Something about haggling over the price of a couple of used wedding rings left a sour taste in Charlotte's throat.

A pink Cadillac ceremony and pawn shop wedding bands, she thought, then shook her head.

The same nagging feeling began to creep up again, and Charlotte tried to reason it away. It had no name, but Charlotte felt its seriousness just the same.

"We were thinking of taking in the dinner show at the hotel before we head over to the chapel," Bill offered. "Whadya say?"

"Oh, I don't think so," Seth quickly replied. "We've got some things to work out before the ceremony. You two go ahead and we'll meet you in the lobby at nine-thirty."

By the time the old man packaged up the rings and processed Seth's credit card, Dyann and Bill had gone on their way.

"Do you want to walk back or shall I grab a cab?" Seth asked her.

"Let's walk."

A thought crossed his mind quickly. Then again. He considered whether to bring it up, then decided he couldn't not know the answer to the burning question.

"Do you want to tell me why you look as if you're about to burst into tears?"

He could see that she wanted to tell him. She wished she could put her finger directly on the emotion that was building into a frenzy inside her, taking her just to the brink of breaking down but never quite crossing over the edge.

"I don't really know."

"Maybe we need to re-think things?" he asked her. He couldn't bear being the cause of the pain he saw in her.

He waited for her to respond and, when she didn't, Seth pointed out a diner on the corner and took Charlotte by the hand. The feel of her small hand inside of his pressed at the center of his chest, leaving an odd sensation there.

"Go ahead and sit anywhere," the waitress called from behind the checkerboard counter. "I'll be right with you."

Seth's hand felt hot against her back as he guided her toward one of the red leather booths near the window.

"You know, Ms. Dennison, we came here to stand up for Bill and Dyann," he whispered to her across the linoleum table. "There's nothing saying we can't do that and go home."

"I know."

"So why do you look like it's your last day on earth?"

"I'm not really sure," she admitted.

A standing well of tears rose inside her hazel eyes, and Charlotte darted her gaze away from Seth and out to the street.

'No, don't look away from me," he asked her, then took her small hand between his two large ones and stroked the tops of her fingers. "Look right here," he said, pointing to his eyes. "Talk to me."

"I guess it's just the whole idea of this being the last wedding I'll ever have, and it's a farce."

"We can call it off, Charlotte. No hard feelings."

He was surprised at how hard that was for him to say.

"But the thing is . . . I never expected to even have one more wedding, so why is this bothering me so much?" she asked. "It makes perfect sense. And it's not like you're some serial killer or anything. Bill's known you for years. I think he'd tell me if you'd ever been in prison or killed a small child or anything, right?"

"I've never killed anyone, Charlotte," he assured her, still rubbing her hand. "And I was only in prison for one term, and it was just armed robbery."

She chuckled a bit in spite of herself, and Seth tenderly wiped away the tears that had fallen down her face with a napkin from the platinum dispenser.

"What can I get you kids?" the waitress asked, oblivious to the personal nature of their conversation.

"Burgers, fries and chocolate shakes," Seth suggested. "Sound good to you?"

"Great," she said.

Charlotte looked at the large-faced clock on the far wall. It was after four.

She muttered something about not having eaten since breakfast, then looked into his eyes so deeply that it jarred him slightly.

"I'm looking at this as a means to an end," he said cautiously. "I see that it will help us both. I'll admit it didn't make much sense at first, but the more I think about it, the more I analyze the possibilities . . . I'm prepared to do this."

He leaned down to capture Charlotte's escaping gaze, then brought her chin upward atop one gentle finger.

"The thing is, if you want out, we'll stop right here and now. Do you?"

She timidly shook her head.

"Then I think we should at least have a little fun with it. We're about to get married in the back of a pink Cadillac, for heaven's sake. If we can't have fun with that . . . well . . . we have no business getting married at a drive-thru chapel in the first place!"

A giggle escaped her throat and she sniffed back the tears that threatened to follow.

"This is not a permanent solution, Charlotte," he said. "Just until we both get a little further in our careers. We could set a maximum, if you'd like, just in case."

"Like five years," she suggested. "It's not like it's an actual marriage, after all. So it wouldn't be an actual divorce, right?"

Seth knew she was trying to convince herself more than convince him.

"We could draw up some papers first, if that would make you feel better about things."

"No," she said. "We don't have to sign anything. I think we're both pretty clear on the ground rules. And how would we word this anyway?"

"You still want to go ahead then?" he asked. "Because I'm okay with it either way. Whatever you decide."

He surprised himself with his sincerity. He cared about this woman, and he didn't want to look back later and wonder if he had manipulated her into anything that might have caused her the slightest amount of pain or concern. Yes, he wanted the travel benefits. And yes, he was willing to offer something she needed in return. But if she was unable to find peace with the arrangement, if there were even the slightest, narrowest doubt in her mind . . . well, then, he didn't want the arrangement at all.

Charlotte heaved a heavy sigh and smiled at Seth.

"I want to go ahead with it," she said finally. "I guess I just need to come to terms with it better."

"You will," he said with a grin that lit up his face and

ignited a fire inside Charlotte's chest. "When you're riding that gondola in Venice, or moving into your new place."

Or when she looked into the graying eyes of her father for the last time, she added silently. She would know, even if he didn't, that she had provided what he needed in his final days—medical care, a roof over his head, the consistency of good nurses.

And dignity, the most important thing. She had considered nearly a dozen other nursing homes before she'd decided on Heathcliffe. It was elegant, charming, and had a homey atmosphere rather than the sterile feeling of a hospital. Charlotte knew her mother would have chosen Heathcliffe.

"Just like I will when I'm flying first class without spending the first twenty minutes of the flight wondering if my Visa is maxed out or if I can manage to charge my hotel in the next city," Seth continued, and Charlotte shook herself back to the present.

The casual way he caressed her hand brought impulses of electricity up from her toes to the base of her tingling skull. He was so businesslike about it all. Their marriage was just another contract with details to iron out. And yet there was a contradicting gentleness about him. Seth was an easy man to care about, an easy companion.

She could see him in her life with no trouble at all, sharing tales of their days, working through tough problems. She could see them taking long walks and talking in bed all hours of the night.

Nestled safely behind the vast blue of Seth Pruitt's eyes, Charlotte could see a future she never dreamed existed. She saw the shadows of an unborn child she never realized she yearned to bear; she saw the pale mauve of a bedroom wall in a home she didn't yet own with him at her side.

Suddenly Charlotte realized what was nagging her. She

knew now precisely why the hair had risen on the back of her neck each time Seth referred to their marriage as one of convenience, a logical solution to mutual problems, the means to an end.

The idea of a marriage of convenience wasn't what was choking her. It was the idea of the separation that would follow.

Chapter Five

When Charlotte had phoned Dyann about what to wear to the wedding, her friend had warned her that it would be "ultra casual." She was glad now that she hadn't limited herself to Dyann's "just blue jeans" suggestion, although she never would have imagined in her wildest dreams it would be her own wedding she'd be dressing for!

The housekeeping department of the hotel provided a battered set of electric curlers, and, although she had planned to pin them up, she rather liked the way the curls looked loose around her shoulders. Charcoal gray eye-shadow highlighted and brought out the deepest green of her eyes, and a bit of liner added a touch of drama.

The black stonewashed jeans fit like a second skin over a white bodysuit with a heart-shaped bodice and lace sleeves and neckline, and she finished the outfit with small white leather ballet-type slippers with tiny leather bows atop each one. She didn't look much like a bride but, if this were just a night out back in Atlanta, she'd have been well pleased.

Charlotte was amazed at her demeanor. Her depression had all but disappeared, and she was almost feeling happy as she prepared for the evening's festivities. She was getting married!

She had such an overpowering urge to call someone! She thought about Lorette, then decided it would be much more fun to tell her in person. She planned to wait until her friend asked about the ring.

"Oh, that," she would say. "Didn't I mention I got married?"

The anticipated knock at the door came just as she was spraying a dab of Jessica McClintock's trademark scent to her various pulse points, and she breathed in the array of white roses, gardenias, and lilies. Seth did the same the moment the door opened.

"Heaven smells like you," he told her, then pulled her close in an embrace, planting a quick kiss on her cheek. "You ready to get married?"

"I am indeed. Just let me get my purse."

They couldn't have looked more coordinated had they actually consulted each other. Seth looked almost elegant in black jeans and tee-shirt topped with an antique-white linen jacket. She could see that he had touched up his silver-tipped black boots, probably with a wet washcloth from the bathroom, and she resolved to teach him the fine art of shoe-shining over the next few years. But for now it was Seth's signature, and she wanted him just that way for their wedding.

"Okay," she said, looking back into the room to see if she forgot anything. "I'm ready when you are."

She hadn't noticed how close they were until she looked up into his blue eyes where he stood in the doorway, his arm casually leaning up over her head and against the wall, and his gaze so strong and steady. The weight of it startled her.

"You are so beautiful," he said, his clear voice taking on a deeper throaty quality. "I'm marrying the most beautiful woman in Las Vegas, and I've never even kissed her yet."

Charlotte swam around in his eyes for what felt like a very long time but could only have been a few seconds before replying.

"We'd better go."

"Charlotte," he whispered, then raised his hand to gently cup her face. She couldn't help leaning into the warmth, and she closed her eyes and nuzzled his palm for a moment before he covered her mouth with his for the first time.

She'd been waiting her whole life for a kiss like this. Deep and powerful, so gripping that she wondered if her knees were going to melt like a candle set out on hot pavement on a summer afternoon. Seth's thumb delicately caressed the side of her face, and she couldn't remember ever being kissed so completely.

Charlotte slid her arms slowly around his neck and wove her fingers into the fullness of the thick, sun-kissed hair at his nape. It wasn't a frantic kiss, one born out of frenzy or need; rather, it was a penetrating kiss, deep and thorough and full.

When they finally parted, both of them were quietly breathless, and they exchanged a look of near-surprise.

"What was that?" Charlotte asked him in a whisper, and then a smile glided across her warm mouth.

"It's what's been inside me ever since we met, I think," he replied honestly.

Sometimes his honesty was sharp, she thought. Any other man she'd ever met would have brushed it off or danced around it, but Seth jumped right on the issue. No holds barred.

"We're not going to start dating after the wedding, are we?" she asked with a giggle, then was sorry she'd been so flip. His silence poked at her like the tip of a sharp, cold knife. "Come on, or we'll be late for our own wedding," she added, handing him a tissue from the box on the table. "You might want to wipe off the lipstick."

"And you might want to repair yours."

One look in the mirror told her that he was right. "I'll just be a minute."

In the bathroom, Charlotte took a moment to re-group. She wondered what in the world Seth was feeling. That kiss was not a platonic, let's-get-married-for-business kind of kiss, and yet he couldn't even manage the thought of seeing more of each other after the wedding. He was a walking contradiction.

As she brushed in the last bit of color inside the lip liner, she noticed him standing in the doorway watching her.

"Almost ready." She tried to smile, but he didn't return it. *Was he having second thoughts*? she wondered.

She itched to ask him what he was thinking just then, but resisted with all her might. She wanted him to make her promises, she realized. Even promises he had no intention of keeping. Promises that would justify the emotions she now recognized.

She *loved* him.

She wanted it to have happened for Seth, too, although she knew it hadn't. And Seth Pruitt was not the kind of man to make a promise he had no intention of keeping.

Charlotte silently cursed him for his integrity. Just for this one night, couldn't he let that halo slip just a bit? Just an inch or two, just for that one night? That one moment?

Dyann and Bill were already waiting in the lobby and, despite the irreverence of their wardrobe, they truly did look to Charlotte like a couple deliriously in love. There was something different about it this time. She couldn't put her finger on it but, as she gazed at her old friend, it was almost tangible.

Both Bill and Dyann were wearing faded jeans and tennis shoes topped off with long-sleeved tee-shirts painted with a tuxedo and a wedding gown, respectively. Deep down she'd always known it, but Charlotte acknowledged right then that her friend would never really grow up completely. She was the direct lineage of Peter Pan, and it was one of the things Charlotte loved about her most.

"Come on, you two!" Dyann called from the doorway. "Wait till you see the car!" And she ran out the door, pulling Bill by the hand toward the bright pink Cadillac convertible parked at the curb.

"Wait!" Seth gasped, then yanked gently at Charlotte's arm. "Flowers! I forgot to get you flowers."

He frantically looked around for a moment, then hurried to the center of the lobby, where he pulled an exotic, long-stemmed white flower from the arrangement and brought it back to her.

By the time they reached the door, Dyann already had some stranger snapping pictures of herself with Bill, then squealed with delight at the appearance of Charlotte and Seth.

"Come over here, you two. Get in the picture!"

"We will need wedding photos," Seth said, then urged Charlotte forward where they posed with their friends, then for some alone in front of the Caddy.

When Seth opened the back door for Charlotte, she gasped with delight as she stepped in, knee-deep in pink and white rose petals.

"Isn't this the greatest?" Dyann called back to her as Bill climbed in and turned over the key.

"Last chance to back out," Seth whispered to her, but she ignored the offer.

Bill cranked up the radio and all four sang along as fragrant rose petals floated out of the car and into their hair and onto their clothes.

"Goin' to the chapel and we're gonna get ma-a-arried. Goin' to the chapel and we're gonna get ma-a-arried. Gee, I really love you and we're gonna get ma-a-arried. Goin' to the chapel of love . . . Yeah, yeah, yeah, yeah, yeah . . . Goin' to the chapel of love . . ."

Charlotte felt almost giddy as Seth slid across the back seat toward her and pulled her close. His arm around her shoulder was the lifeline to him she needed just then.

During the chorus of "Love Me Tender" on an All-Elvis-All-The-Time radio station, Seth raised her face to his and stared deeply into her eyes. When he finally kissed her, electricity spurred them on and shock waves held them together.

This man must have a Ph.D. in kissing! Charlotte thought. A Doctor of Kissology, and Charlotte was his willing student. She wondered if this was one of those gifts bestowed by God, like a talent for painting, making last-minute touchdowns, or . . .

"You guys have to take your shoes off," Dyann called back to them, but they couldn't seem to break the lock that held their gazes firmly on each other. "The rose petals are so great on bare feet!"

After a moment, Seth shrugged and reached down to pull off Charlotte's shoes one at a time, then his own. With a nudge, he pulled her feet up to his lap, and Charlotte leaned happily back on the car door while Seth heaped piles of petals from the floor to cover her bare feet.

"And you were worried I wouldn't have flowers," she called out to him above the radio and the hum of the traffic they passed by.

"How many thousands of roses do you think gave their lives for our wedding?" he called back, and they both laughed out loud.

There was something magical about the night, and Charlotte could tell that they both were feeling it. She rested her head atop the window strip and let the rushing air caress her face and her hair. There was nowhere else on earth she would rather be at that moment than on her way through the brisk desert night in a pink convertible to a drive-thru chapel where she would marry a man she'd loved since the moment she laid eyes on his scuffed shoes in the Atlanta airport.

"I think I love you, Mr. Scuff-Shoe," she whispered to him, knowing full well that he was so engrossed in rubbing her toes with one velvet rose petal that he couldn't possibly have heard her above the roar of the night. "And I may just love you until I die."

Seth couldn't make out what Charlotte had said, and he wondered if perhaps she was just singing along with the radio as he twirled a rose petal around her baby toe and then rubbed it along the ball of her foot.

She seemed so joyful at that moment. Her face betrayed her spirit, and he could see that she had found the peace he had hoped she would find in the bargain they'd struck.

The way the wind tossed her hair around, the way the spontaneous, graceful smile warmed her lips, the easy and relaxed way she leaned back against the door with her green eyes closed . . .

She's so beautiful, he thought.

He couldn't help but wonder for a moment why such a

sensual, delightful creature would be in the back of a pink Cadillac on her way to marry a virtual stranger.

Yes, there was her father, he acknowledged, and the need for the extra money for his care; but certainly there were men swarming around someone like Charlotte, vying for the chance to provide an easier life in return for her love. He imagined the kind of love this woman could give would be genuine and all-encompassing. She was not the kind of woman to love partially or half-heartedly.

Seth's eyes stroked her entire body as Charlotte, unaware of his gaze, stretched back into the wind, her toes curling slightly in Seth's hands. Perhaps she had grown cold toward the idea of marriage as he had, he thought. Once he'd lost Michele, the notion of ever again loving so completely had been washed away and replaced with indifference. Seth saw nothing in the marriages around him now that enticed him to re-think his stand.

He'd been raised in orphanages for the most part, and the various sets of foster parents he'd lived with throughout his early life had exhibited nothing more toward each other than mutual need in their attachments rather than any true passion or commitment. For the most part, marriage seemed unnecessary to Seth—an annoyance, really. A step two people took out of some need, real or imagined, perhaps the end result of two joined incomes or another shoulder to bear the weight of some trouble. Or maybe it was just a simple need for a dancing partner, someone to make conversation with, someone to make the days less lonely; something more primal to fill the nights.

He'd sometimes thought he might like a partner himself if true passion existed rather than the mediocre arrangement he always perceived in other couples, but Seth had come to believe that the real thing existed only in films or books. The closest he'd ever come to true love was Michele, and their story had ended in such tragedy that her memory only served to confirm his suspicions of love. He now possessed an innate desire to keep a healthy distance from it, like a lion spotted while on safari—lovely to look at, but dangerous when confronted.

He watched Charlotte for a long moment, and he couldn't help but smile. There was such a freedom about her, and yet, at the same time, she—like he!—was a prisoner of life and love.

If this were a real marriage, he thought, *there might be a lot we could bring to one another.*

But it wasn't a real marriage, he kept reminding himself. It was nothing but business between them. Anything else would be a huge error in judgment.

A joyous one, yes. But an error just the same.

Chapter Six

The neon sign announced their destination, *Nuptials*, the drive-thru wedding chapel where Charlotte and Seth would take their vows.

Her feet still planted in Seth's lap, she took her time in filling out the paperwork while they waited in line.

"It's as easy as driving through for a Big Mac," she said, giggling, and Seth grinned.

Charlotte's stomach trembled with butterflies as the window attendant collected the cash and paperwork. The *thud!* of the stamp the woman inked to the top of the page with Charlotte's signature reverberated all the way down to her toes.

"This is it," Seth smiled at her, and she returned the squeeze he gave to her hand.

"I have a feeling about you two," Dyann whispered to Seth where he sat behind her. "You're going to fall in love with the idea of being together, you just mark my words."

"Believe her," Bill warned seriously. "She told me on the night we met that I'd want to marry her someday soon. And here we are!"

"Ordering up a McMarriage," Seth quipped, and they all laughed.

"So, this is a double whammy, huh?" the old man who appeared in the window bellowed out to them. "Haven't had a double in a while. You folks ready to do the deed?"

"Are we ever!" Dyann shouted.

Charlotte wanted to look at Seth, but she couldn't summon the courage. She knew she couldn't bear detecting even the barest trace of regret or second thought lingering in his eyes, and so she didn't look. In this case, she decided, ignorance was indeed bliss.

"We are gathered here," the man began without warning, and Dyann rose up in the seat, kneeling excitedly next to Bill, her arms fast around his neck, "to witness the nuptials of two very special couples. Thus, the name." He grinned, then pointed upward to the flashing neon sign forming the arch above their heads.

The man reminded Charlotte of Albert Einstein, the way he peered down at them over the thick eyeglasses perched at the tip of his nose. After shuffling through the paperwork, he continued. "William Stanton Ballard and Dyann Prudence McVay—"

"Prudence?" Seth teased, and Dyann stuck her tongue out at him.

"Billy and Dy," she interjected.

"Billy and Dy," the man repeated dutifully with a crooked grin that showed jagged yellow teeth. Charlotte could hardly suppress the urge to burst out laughing. "And Seth Aaron Pruitt and Charlotte Ann Dennison."

He paused and looked at them over those silly glasses,

and Seth nodded. Charlotte wanted to correct him with "Ms. Dennison and Mr. Scuff-Shoe," but she didn't.

"The very fact that you've chosen these surroundings," he continued, "tells me that you are destined for the magnificent. In marriage, a sense of fun and adventure, a sense of humor, is imperative. If you find you can laugh together, you'll surely love together long after the chemistry goes kaputt."

Charlotte realized just then that one of the things she loved the most about Seth was his sense of humor. She loved the way they could exchange zingers one moment and then talk about something serious the next.

"One word of advice from an old fart who sees more couples drive through than Ronald McDonald?"

Charlotte and Dyann exchanged grins, and she heard Seth chuckle beside her.

"Go for the gusto in this life, children. Look at every blessing as if it were your final one. And appreciate every moment for the gift that it is."

Charlotte felt her heart expand inside her chest, and she braved a quick look at Seth, who gave her one of his broad, full smiles.

"Seize the day," he whispered, then gave her hand a gentle pinch. She didn't know if he meant in general, like marrying someone for extra cash and travel benefits, or if there was more meaning packed into the little squeeze. She hoped for the latter.

"That said," the old man croaked, "do you fellas take these ladies to be your lawful wedded wives? To cherish and treasure and pamper and spoil at every opportunity as long as y'all shall live?"

"I do," they both replied, but Seth's crisp voice stood out in Charlotte's ears like fine crystal on a Sunday morning table.

"And do you two beautiful ladies still want these rascals for your lawful wedded husbands?" he asked, peering at them over the bridge of his glasses. "To love and comfort, to trust and be trusted by, to put up with at all times as long as y'all shall live?"

"I do," Dyann rang out first.

"Yes, I do," Charlotte said, and Seth took her hand softly into his. When their eyes met, she wondered if she was seeing honest emotion, or was it just the rush of the moment?

"Well, if you're sure then," the man stated, shaking his head dramatically, "I guess you folks are hitched."

"Yeeeee-hah!!" Dyann hooted before throwing herself on Bill and kissing every inch of his face.

"You two," the man said to Seth. "That goes for you as well."

It was the first sign of shyness Charlotte had seen in Seth, and she thought she noticed a sudden flush of color rise across his face. He gave her a small smile, then moved toward her in a kiss that started out timidly. As its intensity and depth slowly increased, Charlotte felt him cup the back of her head with both hands tangled into her wind-blown chestnut curls.

Charlotte started to giggle against Seth's teeth as Dyann and Bill began to hoot and clap.

"He starts out slow as molasses in January," the old man behind the window chortled, "but the boy's got the moves!"

"I told you I had a feeling about these two," Dyann announced.

When they finally separated, it was carefully, their gazes locked together, smiles rising to their lips simultaneously.

"So . . . Mrs. Pruitt," Seth said.

"That's Ms. Dennison to you," she replied, laughing, and

he took her in his arms again and kissed her until her toes actually began to curl up.

The ride back to the hotel was silent. Dyann had moved so close to Bill on the front seat that it was a wonder he was able to drive at all, and Charlotte finally settled casually down into the seat with Seth's arm draped loosely around her shoulders.

The radio hummed whispered strains of an old Smokey Robinson number, but Charlotte couldn't remember all the words. She was just glad they'd strayed from Elvis for a while.

Charlotte Pruitt.

She tried it on for size, and it fit maddeningly like a glove.

Seth Dennison.

They even fit backwards.

Being so close to Seth was intoxicating, combined with the brisk night air and the distant scent of wild jasmine. Charlotte had never loved anyone so completely, she was sure of that.

The words of the old man who'd performed the ceremony were like a favorite old song in her memory, and, like a familiar chorus she knew by heart, they sang out clear and strong in her mind.

"Go for the gusto . . . Look at every blessing as if it were your final one."

It was good advice, she decided. Charlotte had been playing it safe far too long. She couldn't remember how everything happened exactly, and she wondered what precise moment it was in which her heart had jumped ship and landed on Seth.

She went over their meeting laboriously in her mind, picking through her memory as if searching for the all-important needle in the proverbial haystack, struggling to put her finger on that exact moment when everything she thought she believed in with all her heart went sailing out the window so effectively.

It must have been his smile, she finally concluded. The way it changed his whole face, and affected those fortunate enough to be in its presence.

She realized just then how she must sound!

Melodramatic! Like a woman in an English film, going on for eons about a man's smile, she thought.

For heaven's sake, she was in love far more deeply than she'd originally thought!

There was a stark reality looming over them—one that ensured that these feelings inside Charlotte were going to be shattered into several gazillion pieces in a matter of mere hours. It was an issue she had no desire to confront just then. Its glaring harshness, however, succeeded in overpowering the moment and brought an instant pool of tears to her eyes.

How am I going to get out of this car and say good-bye, only to go home and just continue to live my life as I did before? she wondered.

Nothing was ever going to be the same again.

"Are you getting hungry?"

She couldn't look up at him and risk exposing the well of emotion brimming inside her. One look from Seth, one shared glance into his eyes, and the dam would surely break.

"Mm-hmm," she murmured, then turned and leaned back against him in one smooth motion.

"We're going to hit the magic show," Bill called back to them. "Why don't you two join us?"

"I'm not much for magic." Seth leaned down and

breathed into her ear. "But if you think you'd like to go, I'll give it a try."

"I'm not interested either." She tried to sound light-hearted, which was very difficult considering how much her heart actually weighed at the moment.

"Just a late supper then," he agreed, then louder for Bill's benefit. "My flight leaves early in the morning."

A quake of disappointment crashed within her.

Now, why did he go and mention it right out loud like that? she thought.

Was he really so anxious to get back to the real world? Because the world she had hesitated to even leave to be present at the wedding of an old friend now seemed so distant, so unreal, that she felt as if she might blink it all away quite easily.

If only . . .

The funny old man at *Nuptials* crossed again over the path of her consciousness, and Charlotte grinned through her standing tears.

"Seize the day," Seth had confirmed, and the little voice in her head was pressing her to do just that.

She wondered how he would react if she acted out this sudden fantasy that was starting to take on a life of its own.

What if . . .

What if she told him how she was feeling? What if she just laid it all out on the table like the crowded contents of her handbag? What then?

"Look, Pruitt," she would say matter-of-factly, "sorry to complicate the proceedings of our arrangement. But the plain truth is that I've found myself riciduously in love with you and, seeing as we're married anyway, perhaps we can re-negotiate our temporary plan for a lifetime contract. What do you say, Pruitt? You game?"

"Is there someone at the hotel who will call the airline

and confirm my flight for me?" he said, interrupting her daydream.

Charlotte sat solidly against him, startled.

"Yeah, I'm sure there is," Bill replied.

Her blood thickened inside her veins. This was what he was thinking about just then? Confirming his flight?

It wasn't bad enough that they hadn't even been married a full hour before he began looking forward to leaving the state, but hadn't it even dawned on the big oaf to ask her to take the same flight back? Or even to wonder when she was planning to leave herself?

"So when do you head out?"

The roar of her own voice inside her head nearly drowned him out.

What, he reads minds?

"About one-thirty tomorrow afternoon, I think," she managed to say. "I have to call and check the flight loads to see where I fit in."

"Ah," he nodded, and she felt him shift a little beneath her. "Maybe you could confirm my flight while you have them on the line. Then we can head down for something to eat."

About that previous fantasy, Pruitt. The one in which I proclaimed my love for you? Never mind.

It seemed like an hour before they finally pulled up to The Excalibur. As she stalked past the costumed crowd in the lobby, Charlotte marveled at the way Seth could take her from swooning to swearing in such an amazingly short span of time.

"Hey!" Dyann called, and she had to run to catch up to Charlotte at the elevator. "Are you all right?"

"Fine," she lied, then forced a smile to her unhappy face and embraced her friend. "Congratulations, Dy."

"You, too."

"Don't be ridiculous," she said as she took a step backward. "Your marriage and mine aren't similar in any way."

"Don't be so sure," she replied, smoothing a lock of Charlotte's windblown hair down into place.

"You want to call the airline from your room or mine?" Seth asked her as he rang for the elevator.

Doesn't his brain ever consider more than one issue an hour?

"Doesn't matter," she muttered.

"Will I see you before you leave?" Bill asked Seth, then moved past the women toward his friend.

"I doubt it. I have to shove off by six a.m."

Six a.m. The hour Charlotte's life would turn back to a big, hollow pumpkin.

"Well, thanks for coming, man," and Charlotte watched as the two of them embraced.

"Thanks to you, too," Bill said to her, and the foursome was suddenly involved in sets of heartfelt good-byes.

"I love you!" Dyann called back to her when she and Bill finally headed toward the lobby, hand-in-hand.

"I love you, too."

She stood in the corner of the elevator and subconsciously twisted the band of diamonds which now encircled her finger. In just a few hours, that ring would be a constant reminder of love . . . lost.

"You two are really good friends," Seth stated.

"Yes. Since we were kids."

"And yet you couldn't be more different."

"I think I could stand to be more like Dyann," Charlotte said truthfully, the bitter taste of regret lingering in the back of her throat. "Maybe then . . ." Her words trailed off into silence.

"Then . . ." he urged her on, but Charlotte didn't expound. "Then what?"

She just shrugged and turned away. The open elevator door was a welcome aid to ending that tack.

"Which way is your room?" she asked, pointing in one direction and then the other, but Seth didn't reply. "Pruitt? To the left or the right?"

When there was still no response, Charlotte turned to face Seth. Something was flashing in his blue eyes, and she noticed it right away.

"Pruitt?"

"Okay, Charlotte."

He seemed angry, and that was confirmed as he firmly pushed her back to the wall and held her there by the shoulders.

"Let's stop playing games here. What is wrong with you?"

Chapter Seven

"What do you mean?" she asked him, knowing full well that he could see straight through her.

"You know what I mean. You've been cold as ice since the ride back to the hotel."

Suddenly, he realized how tight his grip had become, and he looked at her apologetically for a moment before brushing a stray wisp of hair from his brow and re-directing his burning gaze down the long hall beside them.

"Talk to me, Charlotte."

How could she dare speak the words that were racing to the surface of her emotions? How could she tell him how happy she was to be his wife, how very much she wished he loved her, too. How horrible she found the thought of leaving him behind now that she'd just found him.

They were illogical emotions, all the more absurd when she set them to music with the words in her head. She had no right to feel what she was feeling, no right at all since

66

Seth had been perfectly honest about his intentions right from the start. Taking on the title of husband, not the role, had been the bargain—nothing more had even been insinuated. And yet . . .

"Charlotte?"

Oh, how she loved the way he said her name.

"I'm sorry, Seth," she finally replied, and he looked her hard in the eye until she waivered on her feet. "You're right. I know I'm acting like a child, and I've tried to stop myself with no luck at all."

"What are you thinking?" he asked, and she smiled at the thought of unleashing it.

"It's wedding day blues," she told him. "Plain and simple. I'm sorry. Seeing Dyann marrying someone she adores, who worships the ground she walks on right back, it made me realize how much I don't have, that's all. I'm feeling a little . . . lonely, I think. That's it. Then all your talk about your flight, and leaving, and I guess it just brought it home to me that I'm never going to be that happy."

"I thought you said you didn't want that for yourself," he reminded her gently. "You said it wasn't the life you wanted."

"It's not."

Did she imagine the glint of disappointment she saw in him?

Of course you imagined it, she scolded herself.

The look on his face melted to one of confusion, and she chuckled right out loud.

"I know!" she groaned. "It makes no sense at all. Just indulge me, Pruitt. Think of it as my wedding gift."

"I thought I was your wedding gift," he said.

"You are."

If he knew how heartfelt and true her reply was, he'd surely have run screaming from the building!

"I'll try to gain a little perspective, okay?"

"And that's my wedding gift?"

"Yeah," she said, smiling.

When he nodded in the direction of his room, she graciously accepted his extended arm, looping hers through it and quietly following his lead.

Seth's ticket told Charlotte why he hadn't invited her to fly back to the east coast along with him. The next leg of his journey was to San Francisco.

"You're going to California?" she asked as she sat at the edge of the king-sized bed beside the telephone.

"There's a development firm I've done quite a bit of business with. Most of my biggest projects have been for them, as a matter of fact. I got a tip that they've just purchased about thirty acres of land and are planning to put up some low-cost, affordable housing for first-time buyers."

He sat down in the chair across the room and let his ankle rest atop the opposite knee. "I've been working on designs for a similar project for a couple of years now, and if I can sell them this idea it could be a good first step to striking out on my own in the development business."

"Step one being the opportunity to show people what you can do," she said.

"Right. I have a lunch appointment with the CEO tomorrow."

"I'll be keeping my fingers crossed for you," she promised. "I'll say a little prayer that . . ."

Just then, an operator picked up the line on the other end. "Thank you for calling Global Airlines. This is Miss Swanson. How can I help you?"

"Flight 211 for tomorrow morning," Charlotte stated. "Is it running on schedule?"

"Las Vegas to San Francisco, departing at seven a.m.," the woman replied.

"Great." Charlotte nodded at Seth. "Can you check the load on Vegas to Atlanta on the afternoon flight? I'm an employee."

"Certainly."

"It's too bad you couldn't get an earlier flight," Seth told her while the woman checked. "We could ride out to the airport together."

Her heart soared. More than anything, she had wanted him to at least make the suggestion.

"Can you check the morning flight as well?" she asked, and Seth nodded.

"It looks like either one would be good," the woman told her. "You should have no problem on either flight."

"Why don't you list me on the six forty-five then," Charlotte tried to remain casual for Seth's benefit. "Looks like I've got an early ride to the airport."

While she provided all the information necessary to be added to the standby list, Seth busied himself about the room, folding a sweater and zipping it into the brown Samsonite case on the stand, double-checking the contents of his portfolio before closing it and leaning it upright beside the other bag.

Charlotte enjoyed the opportunity to watch him when he didn't realize it. She drank him in, the way he moved, his careless grace. He was such an interesting, beautiful man. As she hung up the phone, he disappeared into the bathroom, and she could hear the clatter of toiletries being rounded up and packed away.

"Do you think we'll need a reservation this late?" she called to him. "I can ring downstairs."

"I doubt it," he replied. "Let's just head down."

"I was thinking I might stop by my room and grab a sweater," she said nonchalantly as she ran a hand over the top of his suitcase. She recognized the barest trace of his scent lingering in the room, and she closed her eyes and breathed in as much of it as she could.

"We can," he said, and she released the breath raggedly as he appeared in the doorway. "Or you can just take my jacket. It's hanging on the hook by the door."

She wandered over to a short black leather jacket with wide silver zippers up both cuffs and cut diagonally across the front. Slipping into it, she stepped up to the mirror on the back of the closet door and examined her reflection.

"It's a little big," he said from behind her, grinning. "But it will do if you'd like."

"Thanks."

She admitted silently that, if she couldn't wrap herself in his arms, his jacket would be her next choice. Her sweater could never compare to the feel of the jacket's cool lining caressing her skin through her lace sleeves or the spicy scent of its owner that still lingered within its fabric weave. She would coil herself inside it and, like the night itself, she would enjoy it for every magical moment that she could.

Moments were, after all, what life was made up of, she realized. And no matter what followed tomorrow, no matter how excruciating it would be to let him go, she was going to appreciate every enchanting instant she could squeeze out of their final hours. And when she finally said good-bye to Seth the next morning, when she finally let him go as she knew she would have to, she would have something wonderful to take home with her.

She vowed that she would not leave Las Vegas empty-handed. She would take with her the memory of their time together. New resolve coursed through her, and Charlotte tingled with the excitement of her mission: To create something tangible to take home. Something so wonderful that she could hold on to it when she began to realize just how very far he was from her.

"Ready?" he asked, and she nodded happily. She was indeed ready.

On their walk down to the restaurant, they found themselves sidetracked by the Fantasy Fair carnival area created just for kids. It only took Seth three tries at the ring toss before he won a small stuffed lion, which he presented to Charlotte with a regal bow. Before they knew it, over an hour had passed and she was overloaded with prizes, from stuffed animals to plastic toys to a glittery crown made of heavy cardboard and pseudo-jewels.

"How will I ever get all this home?" she asked, giggling as she struggled with an unsteady armload. He relieved her of some of the bulkier items as they stepped into the restaurant.

"Table for two," Seth told the hostess. "Well, maybe three. We'll need an extra chair for all this stuff."

Once seated, Charlotte sighed and slid deep into the chair. "That was fun," she told him. "Thank you."

"I could have won you that elephant," he told her with a silly mock-frown, "but I think that balloon game was rigged."

"Well, it's a good thing if it was," she laughed. "I think Global would draw the line at a standby passenger with an elephant!"

"Mommy, loooook!!!"

Before they knew it, their table was besieged with children, all of them gathered around the chair holding the prizes Seth had won.

"Kids," the exasperated mother groaned. "Leave these nice people alone. Come on, let's get the table before your father arrives."

"Did you win all these, mister?" asked the youngest, a

gap-toothed boy no more than four years old who had taken an instant liking to the bright orange lion in the royal robes.

"He sure did," Charlotte answered for him. "And I don't know how I'll ever get them all home. Would you be interested in adopting that lion?"

"You mean it?"

"Brian!" Mom cried.

"I'm serious," she assured the woman. "I'll never get all this on the plane with me. And there's plenty here for everyone."

The five faces lit up as if they'd just met Santa Claus. Six faces, if she counted Seth's reaction.

"Go on and take your pick," she said, and noticed a nod of agreement from Seth. "Except for this one," she added, plucking a rag doll from the midst of the pile. "This one's mine."

She set the doll on her lap, its legs draped lazily over her own, and watched as the oldest girl doled out one toy to each child.

"No, I want the crown!" the littlest girl whined, and they paused to re-negotiate.

"Say thank you, kids," their mother urged them when they were through.

"Thanks, lady!" . . . "Thank you." . . . "I'll give him a real good home."

"So, what's so special about him?" Seth asked when the family had finally moved away.

"Him?" she replied sweetly. "He's just special, that's all."

She lifted the rag doll from her lap and looked him over with a smile. Dressed like a clown, he had sad little eyes despite the huge grin stencilled across his face, and his scuffed shoes were about three times bigger than his feet should have been.

"Mister Scuff-Shoe," she announced, beaming. "Just like you."

Seth cocked his head slightly and studied the limp little guy. "Like me? . . . Thank you very much."

"That's the first thing I ever noticed about you," she confided, placing the doll carefully on the chair beside her.

"My shoes?"

"Yes."

His smile was crooked as he slid away from the table and plopped his foot up on the seat of the chair next to the doll.

"See?" she said with a chuckle.

He shot her a sideways glance and held it for a long moment, which made Charlotte giggle all the more, even after the waitress appeared.

"What'll it be for you two?" the waitress asked.

"I'll have a grilled chicken salad with buttermilk dressing," Charlotte tried to reply seriously, pretending not to notice Seth's cockeyed glare. "And a glass of iced tea, no lemon."

"And you?"

Seth slowly removed his boot from the chair and leaned forward on the edge of the table.

"Steak sandwich with sliced tomato and onion," he said, not taking his eyes off of Charlotte. "And a cup of coffee."

"Cream?"

"Yes, thank you," he replied, then finally looked up at the woman. "Do you know where a guy might get his boots shined around here?"

Charlotte snickered as the woman thought it over. "Around the corner," she replied. "A few doors down."

After the meal, they ordered a brownie sundae, but Charlotte ate most of it.

"Can I order you another?" Seth teased as she scraped the last bit of hot fudge from the side of the bowl.

"Okay," she returned. "But more whipped cream this time." They both laughed.

"How about it? You want to walk over and get my boots shined?"

"It's almost midnight," she pointed out. "Besides, why spoil your image by changing now?"

"You mean you think this is a good look for me?"

"Well, it sure does succeed in getting you girls," she said, laughing. "I mean, you came to Vegas with scuffed boots and you're leaving a married man. Like I always say, 'If it ain't broke, why fix it?' Besides," she continued, "I've sort of gotten used to it." She smiled broadly.

"Yeah, old buddy," he said as he picked up the clown and set him on the edge of the table, "we gotta beat 'em off with a stick, don't we? If only Kevin Costner had been filled in on the secret. Scuffed shoes. Drives women wild. If he'd only have known, he wouldn't have had all that trouble getting girls, huh?"

"Maybe you could write a book," Charlotte said. "Share your secret with the millions who don't have a clue."

"Sort of spread a little bit of my magic around, huh?" he asked, pretending to mull it over. "Nah, why should I? All that power in the wrong hands could end up in disaster."

"You could be right. Better keep it to yourself then."

"I think that's best."

Chapter Eight

Seth pulled out his wallet and laid a twenty on the table beside the check.

"How much was mine?" Charlotte asked, reaching for her purse.

"Did you forget?" he asked with a wave of his hand. "You're the brains behind this partnership. I'm the cash."

"I can pay for my own meals, at least," she objected, but he was firm.

"That reminds me," he said, changing the subject as he rose to his feet and handed her the doll and her purse. "When do I send my first monthly installment?"

She hadn't even thought of that.

"We'll need to exchange numbers and addresses," he pointed out. "And work out a schedule, I suppose."

"It will take a couple of weeks to get you into the system," she said as they headed across the lobby toward the elevators. "I suppose it will all be done by the first of the month. How about then?"

"The first of the month it is then," he agreed. "I'll send my first check on the same day I pay my mortgage each month. Payable to Rent-A-Wife?"

She giggled at that. "Do you want to come up to my room and exchange information?"

"Sounds good," he replied.

The elevator doors slid open, and he guided her in with a firm hand to her back. It was so easy with him, she thought. Being together was so natural, and yet there they went, upstairs to share information having to do with payment schedules and contact numbers.

Odd. And unusual.

"Are you going to take my name?" he asked curiously as she dug for her key. And when she'd found it, he took it and opened the door to her hotel room, waving her in ahead of him.

She hadn't really considered that, and she took a moment to think it through.

"I don't think so," she told him finally. "I didn't take Luke's name the first time."

"I guess in this case it's logical not to," he agreed. "Shall I order some wine?"

"I'd rather have tea," she said as she slid out of his jacket and placed it gently across the back of a chair. "If you order some hot water and condiments, I have a canister of my favorite tea in my bag. I'll make you some."

"I'm not much of a tea man," he replied. "But I'll try anything once."

"I'll keep that in mind," she teased. "You call room service, and I'll dig out the tea."

The vanilla almond blend was her favorite ever since discovering it on the shelves of a little tea house she'd visited outside of London. The rich aroma caressed her senses the moment she popped the lid on the can, and she held it out for Seth to take a whiff.

"It smells like dessert," he said. "The brownie sundae wasn't enough for you?"

"You'll love this."

Charlotte produced a spiral notebook and pen from the leather bag on the stand and brought it over to the table in the corner.

"I'll write down my information first," she began. "Address, phone numbers, seniority date with the company. You'll need that to travel. And I'll need your employment information, social security number, and date of birth. By the way, do you want me to include you for medical coverage?"

"Insurance?" he asked.

"You'll get it for free," she pointed out. "If you don't have any, you might as well take advantage of it."

"I'm paying an arm and a leg for it now," he told her. "You're sure it's free?"

"Spouses are free," she answered, looking up from the notebook with a grin. "You'll get life insurance, too."

"If I make you the beneficiary, you won't knock me off for the pay-off, will you, Ms. Dennison?"

"Make me the beneficiary?"

"Wouldn't they think it funny any other way? Besides, if anything happens to me, you wouldn't get your monthly payments any more. This would even things out."

"Oh." She considered it, then nodded. "Okay."

"Do I get dental?"

"Yep."

"And it's free?" he asked excitedly. "You're not paying into a fund or something?"

"Nope, it's free."

By the time room service arrived, it was Seth's turn with the notebook, and he filled up the page as Charlotte prepared a pot of tea to steep.

"No cream in mine this time," he told her.

"Let me make this the way it was meant to be enjoyed, Pruitt. Just sit back and shut up."

"Yes, ma'am," he replied as she poured a dab of cream from the tiny ceramic pitcher into each stoneware cup.

She knew it would only take one taste for him to be hooked, and she was right. The look on his face once he'd taken the first sip from his cup told her she had a convert.

"Is this the best tea you've ever tasted, Pruitt?"

"I have to admit that it is," he said, taking another sip. "It's great."

"Now lean back and enjoy it."

"Has anyone ever told you that you're very bossy, Ms. Dennison?"

"Never. In all my life. Nope. Uh-uh."

"Why don't I believe you?" He laughed, and she returned a broad smile.

Charlotte lowered herself into the wingback chair by the window, and Seth sat down on the floor, his back resting against the loveseat, and his boot pressed against the leg of the low coffee table in front of him.

"It's nice and easy between us," he stated after several long moments of silence. "Do you notice that?"

"Yes."

His gaze caressed the hot skin on her face, and she fought against the urge to close her eyes and enjoy the touch of it.

"I've never been so comfortable before with someone I knew so little about," he told her softly.

"I know what you mean," she replied, taking a long sip from the cup cradled in both hands.

The dim light from the lamp on the nightstand cast a pale yellow glow over them, and Seth smiled at Charlotte sweetly.

"Come here."

She thought it over for one quick moment before setting her cup down on the table and approaching him. When he reached up for her hand, she gave it to him without hesitation, and she obediently followed as he pulled her down to his lap. Once she was there, he immediately encircled her in his arms, and she nestled her face sideways into the crook of his throat while he rested his chin on the top of her head.

"You won't be easy to say good-bye to, Ms. Dennison," he whispered.

Then don't say it.

"Have you thought about saying good-bye to me?" he asked her curiously, and she nodded her head quietly.

"You know . . ." she managed after a moment, and her smoky voice trembled a little. She wondered if he'd noticed. "It's not like we won't ever see each other again though . . . is it?"

She clamped her eyes tightly shut and waited.

Here's your chance, Pruitt. Make me an offer. Any offer.

"I suppose not," he finally replied, but he didn't follow it with anything besides silence.

That's it?

"An ongoing relationship wasn't really part of the original bargain, was it?" he continued.

Charlotte wondered if he was awaiting a reply or if that had just been a rhetorical statement.

Just one glimmer, Pruitt, she thought. *If you'll just give me one glimmer of hope that you'd be open to something more . . .*

But in the silence that lingered, the glimmer never came.

* * *

Dawn found them curled up side-by-side on the floor in front of the loveseat, Charlotte's head cupped delicately in Seth's hand, his fingers woven into her hair. She lifted her head slowly and felt the slight pull as her hair threaded free.

Pausing for a moment to caress the gold band that encircled his ring finger, she then ran one gentle finger along his jawline and into his sunstreaked hair.

"I love you so much," she whispered, then planted a breath of a kiss on his unresponsive lips.

Charlotte rose carefully from the floor and stretched. The digital clock on the nightstand flashed 5:04.

"Seth?" she whispered as she squatted down beside him. "Seth."

"Mmmmm."

He began to stir and, when he opened his eyes to focus on her face, she thought that the whole world had awakened at the very same moment. How beautiful those eyes were!

"It's after five," she told him. "We need to get to the airport."

Once Seth was up and moving, they made arrangements to meet down in the lobby in twenty minutes. Although she wanted to try for a quick shower, she knew there wasn't time, and she hurried about the room packing up the last of her personal items—the watch off the bureau, the tin of tea on the table.

She quickly brushed her teeth and used a cloth to scrub the makeup from her face before slipping into a tea-length cotton dress in a muted floral print and a pair of sandals that laced around her ankles. It took just two minutes to apply foundation and lip gloss before she placed the small cosmetics bag in the leather satchel and hurried back into the room.

Her eyes fell quickly upon Seth's leather jacket where it lay draped over the back of the chair, just as she'd left it. Charlotte fought back the wave of emotion that passed over her just then and quickly snatched up the jacket along with her bag and hurried from the room.

Checkout was fast and painless, and Seth had a cab waiting at the door when she was through.

"Airport, please," he instructed the driver, then turned to Charlotte. "You have your notebook, right?"

"Yes. And you tore the sheet out with my information on it?"

"Right here," he nodded, patting the breast pocket of the brown tweed sport coat he had changed into.

"Oh! Your jacket!" she cried, pulling it out from where it was threaded between the handles of her bag.

"If you'd like to wear it," he began, then trailed away to silence. "If you're cold."

"I am a little cold," she admitted. "You wouldn't mind?"

"You can send it to me," he suggested. "Or save it until we see one another again."

Was that a glimmer?

"Seth, I just want you to know . . ." But just what she wanted him to know, she wasn't exactly sure. "I . . . uh . . . Thanks for Mr. Scuff-Shoe," she finally finished.

"You have him?"

"Packed in my bag."

"And the papers from the ceremony?"

"Packed," she replied. "I'll send copies to you."

"Okay," he said as he stared out at the passing scenery. "Whenever you have time."

By the time Seth checked his bags at the curb and they made their way inside the airport to the gate, Charlotte's flight had already pre-boarded. The customary long wait for her name to be called was uncharacteristically short, and she was handed a boarding pass and called to the gate long before she was ready.

"Well." Seth sighed offhandedly, and they looked at each other for a long, awkward moment.

"Well," she repeated.

"Do I thank you?" he said, laughing, and Charlotte shrugged before he pulled her into a slightly wooden embrace. "Thanks for marrying me."

"Thanks for having me," she returned as tears spilled down her face with no forewarning at all.

Seth held her by the shoulders and looked her squarely in the eye, then smiled as he wiped away the tears. She thought she noticed a slight cock-turn of his head. Had her tears really confused him? Could any man be so dense as this one?

"Take care," he told her, and she softly nodded her head.

"You, too."

"Miss Dennison?" the gate attendant called, and Charlotte managed a smile for Seth.

Just as she was set to turn away, Seth pulled her into his arms and lowered his mouth over hers in a tender kiss. Charlotte dropped her bag and his leather jacket to the floor and threw her arms around his neck, returning that kiss with all her passion.

"Miss Dennison, please?"

When they parted, Seth gave her the final gift of his smile, something she had come to treasure so much.

"Bye," she said.

"Good-bye."

Charlotte gathered her things and hurried toward the gate. After one last glance back at him, she turned away and boarded the flight. And she didn't care who was looking as she threw herself into seat 2-A, sobbing beyond control.

Chapter Nine

It wasn't the way she'd planned it, but Charlotte didn't care. She was going to tell Lorette the whole crazy story, and she couldn't—*wouldn't!*—wait until they were at work to do it.

Despite the late hour, she pulled into the driveway of the hacienda-style house and hurried to the door. The moment Lorette appeared, sleepy and somewhat confused, Charlotte burst into tears.

"What is it, honey?" Lorette cried, pulling her robe together with one hand and urging Charlotte inside the door with the other. "When did you get back? Are you all right?"

"Nooooo!" Charlotte wailed.

It took nearly an hour for the whole tale to unfold, and Charlotte told it in so many bits and pieces that her friend had a hard time fitting the puzzle properly together.

"Well, this is a good thing, isn't it?" Lorette asked in a

motherly way. "That you feel something for him after all? I told you you'd meet someone fabulous eventually."

"Baby?"

The women looked up to find James standing in the kitchen doorway, his dark brown chest bare atop loose-fitting pajama bottoms, and rubbing his swollen eyes.

"What's going on? Is that Charlotte?"

"Hi, James," she groaned, then slid her head down into her folded arms atop the butcher block table.

"Did I hear you say you . . . got married?"

"Yes," she moaned to the table surface.

"And now she's in love with him," Lorette filled him in.

"Well, that's great! . . . Isn't it?"

"That's what I've been trying to tell her."

"But he doesn't love me back," Charlotte roared. "Don't you two get it? For heaven's sake, he doesn't love me back!"

"Does he know how you feel?" James asked, and Lorette shook her head. "Why doesn't she tell him?"

Both women shot him a "you've got to be kidding" look, and James tossed his hands helplessly into the air.

"Okay," he said with a sigh. "I'm going to bed. You let me know in the morning if we're going to celebrate this marriage or ignore it. Whatever you decide is all right by me."

"Night, baby."

"Good night, James."

"The girl gets married and you'd think that'd be good," he muttered to himself as he headed back toward the bedroom. "Tell him you love him, I say, but they look at me like I just ran over the dog. I don't know what's up with these women . . . I gotta get some sleep. I'll probably get it tomorrow. I'm missing somethin' here. Heck if I can figure out what it is . . ."

"He is one fine-looking black man, isn't he?" Lorette said, and Charlotte rolled her eyes and fell back into her arms on the table. "Okay, now, girl. You've cried your eyes out and got it all off your chest. Now I want details. What does the boy look like? How's he kiss?"

"Like an angel," she said with a sigh.

"The face or the kiss?"

"Both. He's tall, about six feet, I'd guess. He has this very light brown hair with golden streaks in it. And these incredible blue eyes. He reminds me a little of Hugh Grant." She grinned sweetly. "You know the way his smile changes his whole face? And Lorette, he's got these truly amazing hands . . ."

"Hands?"

"Strong," she explained as she held out her own hand and turned it over in front of her. "And yet gentle."

"Oh, yeah, girl. You've got it bad, haven't you?"

"Yes," she said, then dropped her head one more time.

"You want to spend the night?"

"No," Charlotte said apologetically. "I'll go home. I just needed someone to talk to."

"So when are you two going to see each other again?"

"Who knows. At the divorce hearing?"

"You mean you made no plans to see each other again?"

"Did I mention he lives in New York?" Charlotte muttered.

"New York?" Lorette repeated. "Oh . . . honey."

The first few days were the worst. Filling out the paperwork, telling people at Global all about the sudden wedding. The friend of a friend. The instant connection. The last-minute ceremony. But once she crossed over the rough road, the butterflies inside her stomach eased up, and the tears were not so quick to rise up in her eyes at the mere mention of his name. Things, surprisingly, returned to normal.

As the weeks went by, Lorette and James were instrumental in Charlotte's healing process. They invited her to dinners, trips to the hardware store, a movie here or there. Sometimes she'd spend the night and stay up long after they'd gone to bed, re-reading the letter Seth had included with his first month's check, and she'd silently mouth the words as she did.

Hi, Ms. Dennison.

Enclosed please find your first installment on our marriage. And I promise you it won't bounce. Did you ever wonder if we'd have told that old guy at "Nuptials" what we were really up to whether he'd have included that in the vows?

"Do you promise to issue no bad checks, to always make your payment on time . . ."

I do!

The meeting in San Francisco was amazingly productive, and it looks like the project is all but mine. Waiting for the final word and contracts, but the green light is on.

By the way, do I have health benefits yet? I'm going to let mine go if you don't have any problem with that. I got the premium bill this week and found a certain sadistic pleasure in tossing it into the circular file in the garage. Thanks for that!

Have you heard from the other members of our wedding party yet? Not a word on this end. They're probably off taming some wild animals or spearheading a revolution somewhere, no doubt. Nothing mundane in their futures, I predict.

Mine is another story. It's back to work. Spend this

money well, wife of mine. And let me know when "our" address has changed. Until then, all my love.

Seth Pruitt
a.k.a. Mr. Charlotte Dennison

She still hadn't cashed the thing. She just carried it with her in her wallet, and pulled it out every so often to look at, or run a finger over, the smoothness of his signature.

Enough was enough, she finally decided that night while re-reading the letter for what was surely the thousandth time. Not only was she going to cash that check he'd sent, but she was going to spend it, too! Charlotte vowed to herself right then and there that the very next morning over breakfast she was going to begin studying the classifieds. The first morning of her search for the perfect house.

She'd been waiting a very long time for the day she could finally notify Mrs. Bernard that she would be moving out. The woman was kind, and she'd rented her the single apartment over the garage at the back of her rambling country estate for a price that was more than fair, but Charlotte had quickly outgrown the space and had begun to yearn for a home of her own.

She kept her vow, and that afternoon after work she was combing the streets in Roswell in search of Cottage Lane. It had been her tenth phone call or so, and it had sounded perfect to her, even down to the address. Two bedrooms, a large gourmet kitchen, dining area, patio, fenced yard, $700 per month with an option to buy, utilities paid, pets okay. Charlotte didn't have any pets, but decided that if this was the house for her, she might consider adopting a dog!

The moment she stepped inside the house, an unexpected wave of emotion swept over her. Not only was this undoubtedly the house she'd been dreaming of, but it was suddenly the one she wanted to live in—with Seth.

Aren't you ever going to wake up? she asked herself. *Seth is not your husband in any way besides name only. Get on with your life!*

The master bedroom was roomier than her entire apartment, and the brick patio off the breakfast room was just begging for a gardener's touch. The backyard was surrounded by a whitewashed picket fence, and a brick barbecue that needed a little elbow grease was nestled diagonally into one corner of the yard.

The kitchen graced a good-sized greenhouse window where her herb garden was sure to thrive, and the carved wooden shelves that went around the circumference of the room would be perfect for cookbooks, canisters, and her collection of baskets. She'd have to add furniture as she could afford it, but that would be fun, and she happily left the house two hours later—$1,500 poorer, but with the set of silver keys to her brand-new home.

She could hardly wait to shower and get over to Lorette's to tell her the good news. Her friend had been especially tedious about this particular evening, reminding her several times at work that this dinner party was very important to them, and it would be a rather formal affair. They were hosting James's boss and his wife, along with the administrator of the department, and they needed an even number. Charlotte wasn't sure why it was imperative to Lorette that she be that final guest, but she supposed it was out of pity.

Charlotte couldn't wait to see the look on Lorette's face when it registered that her friend had actually rented a house and was getting on with her life after so many weeks of pathetically moping around. She stood in front of her tiny closet, debating about what to wear as she played the messages that were beckoning from the machine.

Beeeep. "Hi, sweetie. It's Lorette. Just a reminder about tonight. My house, seven-thirty. We've decided on a Mexican theme in case you'd like to dress accordingly. If not, that's okay, too. Please be on time, Charlotte. Seven-thirty, okay? Okay. See you tonight then."

Beeeep. "Char! How are you? This is Dyann. I was just calling to see if you'd received the pictures yet and to see what's up with you and Seth. It was quite a wild time in Vegas, wasn't it? I'm so glad you came, Char. Your being there made it perfect. Billy sends his love, and we'll talk soon. Bye!"

Beeeep.

The pictures? Charlotte didn't check her mail on the way in. She galloped down the outside stairs to pick it up. Sure enough, amongst the bills and flyers and a card from her cousin, there it was. A thick envelope addressed to her in Dyann's recognizable handwriting. She slumped slowly to the stairs and set the stack of other mail down beside her.

The first glimpse of him set her heart to pounding.

The Cadillac hadn't been as pink as it appeared in the photos, and she thought Dyann looked happier than she'd seen her in all their years of friendship. She flipped the pictures over, one after the other, until she reached the final one, where she paused. The last picture in the pile was one she hadn't realized had been taken. The perspective was from the front seat to the back of the pink convertible. Charlotte and Seth kissing, in a rather passionate embrace.

She looked closely at the photo. Seth's hand cupped her head in that certain way she'd forgotten. Several loose rose petals were scattered through her hair, and one was on her shoulder. Charlotte realized it must have been snapped just moments after they were declared . . . husband and wife.

The term stuck in her throat even without saying it out

loud. She glanced down at the band of diamonds on her hand, and then again at the final photo.

Oh, how she missed him.

She had no idea how long she'd been sitting there on the stairs looking at that picture when she heard the phone ringing upstairs. With a start, she shook her head and rose to her feet, taking the steps two at a time as she ran for the phone.

"Hello?"

But the caller had hung up, and she'd forgotten to flick the answering machine back on after listening to Dyann's message. A sudden little voice told her it could have been Seth calling just then, but she dismissed it, tossing the packet of mail onto the bed and hurrying back to the closet.

If Lorette's Mexican fare was anything like her Cajun specialties, the white dress she had planned to wear would surely be at the dry cleaner the next day, and so she opted for a hunter green tank dress topped with a bright multi-colored bolero jacket and red heels that matched the over-sized buttons on the jacket.

Just before heading out the door, she tied her hair with a green silk scarf and fastened it in a bow at the top of her head, adding bulky earrings and an array of festive brace-lets. In the car on the way over, she made a mental note to get Lorette alone as soon as she possibly could to show her the photos Dyann had sent. She could hardly wait for her friend to get a load of the blue eyes and warm smile she'd been droning on about for nearly a month.

The line-up of cars on the street let Charlotte know that the party had turned out to be much larger than originally planned, and she had no doubt that Lorette was up to the challenge. She gave wonderful parties, the consummate hostess, and Charlotte made up her mind to enjoy this one from the start. With the photos in her purse alongside the keys to her new home, she was feeling exceptionally festive this night anyway. It was a perfect evening for a celebration.

She stopped outside for a moment to smooth the front of her skirt and wondered if the hem was too short for this type of business gathering. Charlotte was fairly leggy anyway, but this skirt enhanced that quality all the more.

"Hey, you're here!" Lorette cried when she answered the bell, then quickly opened the door wide. "Come on in."

"SUR—PRISE!!!"

The moment she stepped inside, Charlotte felt woozy, as if she might faint.

What in the world is going on?

Countless friends from Global Airlines moved in toward her, and Lorette was grinning from ear to ear. It wasn't until she saw the banner over the stairway that she understood.

"CONGRATULATIONS, CHARLOTTE & SETH!" it said.

"What's going on?" she asked Lorette over someone's shoulder who was giving her a hug.

"It's your engagement-slash-wedding party," she cried.

"What?"

Brightly colored balloons floated at the ceiling dangling curls of white, red, and green ribbons in the air. The large round oak table in the foyer which normally held fresh-cut flowers was now brimming with wrapped gifts and stacks of cards.

"What have you done?" she asked Lorette, but her only response was a wide "I've-just-eaten-the-canary" smile. "Lorette, for heaven's sake . . ."

"And now for your big surprise!" someone shouted, and the crowd seemed to "ooooh" and "aaahhh" as people stepped aside to create an opening in their midst.

"Happy one-month anniversary, Ms. Dennison," Seth said with a crooked grin, and Charlotte thought she might indeed faint.

"Pruitt . . . What are you . . . doing here?"

"Lorette tells me it wouldn't be good to throw a party for a newly married couple with only half the couple in attendance."

Charlotte looked from Seth to Lorette and back again. She couldn't speak, and her knees felt just moments away from buckling.

"Kiss her!" someone shouted!

Applause roared like thunder as Seth took Charlotte into his arms and did as he was told.

Chapter Ten

"What were you thinking?" she asked Lorette in a whisper, and then they both smiled as Mildred from Human Resources passed through in search of a corkscrew.

"You wanted to see him again, didn't you? I just arranged it for you."

"But how?"

"I stole your address book one night when you were sleeping over, and I copied down his phone numbers and address. Then I called him, said I wanted to surprise you, asked when he could make it in and, *voila!*, we had a party."

"Oh, Lorette . . ."

"Just relax and enjoy, my friend. He thinks he's doing the polite thing to keep your little secret from the people you work with, and you have him all to yourself for the entire weekend."

A smile crept up and covered her entire face. "The weekend?"

"Girl, if you want this man to fall for you, proximity is your only disadvantage. In light of that fact, I have traded your days for you, and you have forty-eight glorious, fun-filled hours of nothing but time. Time in which to show him what we all know already—that you are fabulous!"

Loud music suddenly commenced, and they could hardly hear each other.

"Is that a mariachi band?" Charlotte said, laughing.

"Nothing but the best tonight," Lorette replied with a grin. "Nothing but the best."

"But your neighbors! They're awfully loud . . ."

"I've taken care of that as well," she explained. "I've invited them all to join us. So if someone you've never met wishes you well on your new marriage, it's probably just one of my neighbors. James says there's an unwritten rule that you don't complain about how loud a party is when you're invited to it."

"You're amazing." Charlotte shook her head, then pulled her friend into an embrace. "Thank you."

"Ah," she said as they parted, and Charlotte looked up in time to catch sight of the wink Lorette shot at Seth. "And there he is now. Go, girl. Spend some time with that gorgeous new husband of yours." And before they knew it, the newlyweds were alone in the kitchen.

"Would you like a margarita?" he asked, stretching out his hand toward her.

"I can't believe you're here," she said as she took it, and goosebumps rose on her arms as he led her through the hall and out to the veranda.

The band was set up in the corner of the landscaped yard, and colorful lanterns were strung about them as they played. Seth walked over to the ceramic tile bar and picked up two glasses from the tray, then led her over to one of half a dozen tables on the patio donned in bright green paper tablecloths with small red candles glowing from the center of each one.

"Oh!" Charlotte squealed, then reached inside her purse for the pictures Dyann had sent. "The pictures from Las Vegas."

Seth smiled as he filed through them, then lingered over the last one in the stack.

"When you speak with her," he said, then downed a swig from his glass, "ask her to send me some copies of these, would you?"

"Yes." She was pleasantly surprised that he wanted them.

"I'd forgotten how beautiful you are," he said softly, and Charlotte flushed a bit with color.

"I hadn't."

"What?!" And his grin was crooked.

"I mean you. I hadn't forgotten how beautiful you are."

"Why, Ms. Dennison. Are you flirting with me?"

"I believe I am," she said, smiling. "Call the cops."

Without another word, Seth rose from his chair and led Charlotte by the hand out to the backyard where several couples were dancing to a rhythmic Latin beat beneath lines of burning lanterns.

They were magic together, never missing a single beat. They danced together as if they had been doing so all their lives, and when Charlotte came back to him following several twirls, he gathered her into his arms and dipped her low to the ground. When he raised her back up, she was dizzy, and he kissed her in a way that intensified the feeling.

"I'm woozy, Pruitt." She was breathless as he held her close to him and moved to the beat of the music.

"You ain't seen nothin' yet, Ms. Dennison."

Charlotte wasn't sure what she could possibly do to thank Lorette for the sensational surprise, but she knew she had to think of something. Perhaps giving her firstborn to her.

When almost everyone had gone home and the caterers were clearing out the last of the trays of nachos, enchiladas, burritos, and mini-tacos, Charlotte and Seth said their good-byes to their hosts.

"James picked me up at the airport," Seth told her as he tossed the strap to the familiar garment bag over his shoulder and they headed across the damp lawn. "So I don't have a car. And they naturally assumed I was staying with you. If you can give me a ride to a nearby hotel . . ."

"Do you want to see something first?" she asked excitedly, then led him by the hand to the lone black Toyota at the curb two houses down.

It took less than fifteen minutes to arrive at Charlotte's new home in Roswell.

"Is this where you live?" Seth asked as she produced the keys and opened the door.

"Not yet," she replied, smiling. "But soon."

Seth followed her inside the empty house and waited in the living room while she rummaged for the flashlight she remembered was there. Then, with the help of its yellow stream, she located the switch and flicked on the ceiling fan light in the breakfast room.

"So this is what my money buys in Atlanta," Seth said. "When do you move in?"

"Whenever I'm ready. I rented it today."

"Rented?"

"Well, leased. With an option to buy in the future. Isn't it perfect?"

"I think so. From what I can make out."

"Take my word for it. It's perfect," she said. "There's a

brick barbecue in the backyard, and the kitchen is enormous. Come look."

With the flashlight, she found the switch and flooded the room with light.

"It's the house I've always wanted," she told him as she looked around happily. "I can't believe I forgot to tell Lorette about it tonight."

"I'm glad for you, Charlotte." And he seemed to really mean it despite the tone of sadness she sensed behind it.

The way he looked at her just then ignited a flame inside her heart.

"What is it?" she asked him.

"Let's watch ourselves here, Charlotte," he said slowly, deliberately. "Think. We need to keep our heads."

"I beg your pardon?"

It's just a house, Pruitt. I'm just showing you my house.

"Let's just move slowly."

Move slowly? How much more slowly can we go?

Charlotte looked into his eyes and saw something alarming, and the weight of his words came down on top of her full force. She realized for the first time what she hadn't been able to completely grasp before.

Seth needed her. He needed her travel benefits to make his business a success, and he needed to be married to her to get them. It had never been about her alone, not even for a moment. There was no turmoil within Seth about getting involved with her, she realized now, because he'd known all along that getting serious would never happen. It was only she who kept that futile possibility alive in her heart, hoping he was feeling some of what she felt. And now it was clear that he could look inside her and see that hope.

"Charlotte—"

"No, Seth," she interrupted as she nervously pressed the

front of her skirt with the palms of her hands. "Don't explain. I think I get it now. I'm right back in line where you want me, and I know what's what between us. Don't give me a second thought. It's strictly business from here on out. Don't you worry about a thing."

With that, she flicked out the kitchen light and stormed out toward the front door, leaving him standing there in the dark.

"Charlotte, would you wait a second?"

After just an instant, she heard a thud, and he groaned immediately afterward.

"I can't see a bloody thing, Charlotte!"

She coolly stepped outside and strode across the front lawn. She pulled open the passenger door and, leaving it rocking open, walked around to the driver's side of her car. "If you want a ride to the nearest hotel," she declared to him when he stood in the doorway rubbing his shin, "I'd suggest planting that butt of yours in this car right now. Otherwise, you're on your own, Pruitt."

"Would you let me explain what I meant?"

"I hope you don't think I'm kidding," she continued. "Now, are you staying here and sleeping in that empty house, or are you coming with me now?"

Seth stood in the doorway for a long moment. He seemed to be waiting for the night sky to answer his dilemma, and Charlotte thought it must have replied because he suddenly slammed the front door to the house and stalked down the driveway toward her.

"You really are a piece of work," he said as he leaned down toward her through the passenger door.

"Are you getting in or walking?" she asked in icy anger. "Make up your mind."

"If I tried to sit down in that car next to you right now, every bone in my body would freeze to stone in revolt," he stated as he snatched the garment bag out of the back seat, then slammed the door shut and stomped across the driveway, and down the lawn.

Charlotte sat there for a long moment, her hands clamped so tightly around the steering wheel that they ached. He'd hurt her in the deepest way possible, and *he* was the one leaving *her* behind? And he said *she* was a piece of work?

Suddenly it dawned on her that Seth had no idea where he was going. Despite the overwhelming urge to just drive off and leave him there to forge his own way in the strange and unfamiliar jungle of Roswell, Georgia, she couldn't allow herself the indulgence. She heaved a deep, ragged sigh before turning over the key.

"Would you just get in the car, Pruitt?" she called as she rolled down the passenger window and drove slowly along beside him.

"Just drive away, Charlotte."

The tone of his voice chilled her to the bone. It was laced with something so dismissing. So final.

"You're going the wrong way," she said, a bitter chuckle escaping. "Would you just get in this car?"

He stopped for an instant, then turned on his heels so quickly that it startled her. In her rearview mirror, she watched him walk away, and he looked oddly childlike to her, with his luggage tossed over his shoulder, heading from the street—like a well-dressed little boy running away from home. She watched him helplessly through the mirror's reflection until his form dissolved into the darkness.

"Pruitt."

Tears clouded her vision as she finally peeled away down the street, leaving a spray of gravel and dust in her wake.

Charlotte tossed and turned in her bed for hours. For long intervals, she berated herself for leaving him there, then would remind herself regularly that Seth was ultimately the one who had walked away, not her.

She thought about calling Lorette, or maybe even driving over, but she couldn't bear it. How could she tell her friend—at least tonight!—that her finest attempt at match-making had been botched so miserably.

"Ohhhhh!" Charlotte squealed again at the thought of it, and she buried her head in the pillow deeply until she was hardly able to breathe. She was embarrassed. And angry. And so resentful!

The notion to go and find him glimmered across her mind for the umpteenth time since she'd climbed into bed, but again she talked herself out of it. She wouldn't know where to find him. And what was there to say even if she did?

She allowed the memory of the music at the party to waft gently in her head for a few minutes, and she closed her eyes tight to summon the pictures that went with it. He had held her so close as they danced to that music just a few hours earlier.

Charlotte glanced over at the bureau next to the closet door. Even through the darkness, she could make out the picture Dyann had sent, the one of them kissing at the wedding. No one could know the effect that it had on her, how vividly she could summon up the memory of that kiss and the others that had followed.

She suddenly remembered clearly why she had decided never to marry again. Torment like this was the reason, what she had wanted to avoid by entering a ridiculous marriage with a total stranger!

She began to doze while thinking of his cool dismissal of her, remembering how he had so easily walked away. More willing to face the unknown than to stay and work it through or talk it out.

She fell deeply into sleep while praying that she didn't wake up the next morning to headlines announcing Seth Pruitt and the mysterious accident that occurred while he was wandering around the residential streets of Roswell.

Please God, she thought as she yawned sleepily. *No film at eleven.*

Chapter Eleven

"How could you just drive away and leave him there? Are you nuts?" Lorette cried for at least the dozenth time.

"I don't know!" came the standard reply.

"Baby, how many times are you going to ask her that?" James interjected. "And how many times will she have to tell you she doesn't know?"

"I looked into my mirror," Charlotte explained, wide-eyed and still surprised at her own reaction. "I saw him walking away and I snapped. I just left."

"He could be hurt," Lorette said. "Or worse."

"Oh, thank you," Charlotte grumbled. "That makes me feel so much better."

"Honey, I don't think that's helping the situation," James said, but he fell silent when he was met by Lorette's signature glare. "Okay," he replied as he left the room to answer the convenient chime of the doorbell. "Ooooo-kay!"

"I couldn't believe he just turned on me that way," Charlotte told her friend. "He said he couldn't even stand the thought of sitting near me in the car, and he just started walking."

"That's not exactly the way it happened."

Lorette spun around atop the barstool so sharply that she nearly fell off, and Charlotte felt her entire body turn to glass when she saw Seth standing in the doorway.

"Which part did I get wrong?" she spat at him. "The part where you wouldn't get in the car, or the one where you stormed off like a child?"

"First of all," he explained, sauntering into the room with maddening grace, "I believe what I said was that if I tried sitting next to you in that car my entire body would freeze up in revolt."

"Oh, excuse me. You're right. I was so far off."

"And if anyone was acting like a child last night, Ms. Dennison," he said, "it was you."

"I think I hear James calling me," Lorette said quietly, and she tiptoed out of the room.

"Why did you come back here?" Charlotte asked him. "These are my friends. Not yours."

"I came here," he said sternly, turning her around on the barstool and holding her by the shoulders, glaring into her eyes, "to find you. I had no other frame of reference about where to look besides an empty house you haven't moved into yet and an address where the landlady told me you'd been gone since early this morning. It was either here or the Global Airlines building downtown."

"You went by the Bernards'?"

"Yes, and I met Mrs. Bernard's basset hound up close and personal, thanks very much."

Charlotte held back a snicker. "Schnoodle can be very intimidating, I'll admit."

"He is especially fond of pant legs."

"I've heard that about him," she replied, then recovered a smile that tried to escape.

"Charlotte," Seth continued as he moved close to her. "I can't stand thinking that I hurt you. All I was trying to say was that we need to be cautious with our next move. Treat our relationship with care. Can you understand that?"

She didn't flinch but just watched him, soaking up his words.

"I think we need to see where we're headed."

She dreaded the flow of tears she felt rising with her emotions.

"I care for you, Charlotte."

"You do?"

It embarrassed her how childlike—even hopeful—the words sounded.

"Yes. And if you hadn't been so busy exploding like a rocket on the Fourth of July last night, I could have told you that I'm beginning to feel things for you. Things I can't explain or keep under wraps. Charlotte . . ." He raised her chin atop one finger as he looked into her eyes. "I'm nuts about you."

She froze for a long moment, too still to even feel the flutter of heartbeats that were running wildly into each other, one after another inside her chest.

"You're nuts about me?"

"Yes, Ms. Dennison. You drive me nuts." He smiled.

"That's not what I asked, Pruitt. You said you were nuts about me, right? You're nuts about *me*?"

Seth took a deep breath and narrowed his blue eyes at her.

"I'm certifiable."

Charlotte hopped down from the stool and threw herself full-force into his arms. Seth lifted her off the ground and twirled her around once before setting her back down on the barstool. Looking her squarely in the eye, he put both hands on her shoulders.

"But we're on sandy ground here," he said. "I don't want to make any mistakes."

Charlotte nodded, wide-eyed, as if she were in full agreement. But, if the truth be told, she wasn't entirely sure what he meant.

But what now? she asked herself, then swallowed the wonderings beneath his unexpected kiss.

When James suggested "Char's favorite restaurant" for dinner, Seth jumped on the chance to go.

"I'm in the mood for a celebration tonight," he told them, saving a secretive smile for Charlotte's eyes only, and she went reeling beneath the weight of it. "And I'd like to experience a place known to Georgians as my wife's favorite restaurant!"

But when he saw the sign over the door outside, he had second thoughts.

"Macaroni Grill?" he read, then looked at them.

Glancing down at his attire—a pair of dark jeans and a denim shirt topped with a tweed sport coat and tie—a quiver flickered at the corner of his mouth.

"Am I overdressed?"

"Don't be so judgmental," Charlotte teased, taking him by the hand and leading him through the large wooden door. "Not everything is as it seems on the outside. Of all people, Pruitt, you ought to know that by now."

The innocence of her smile, the way she clasped his hand into hers, the enthusiasm sparking through every inch of her—she intrigued him. He felt like a kid in a candy store with Charlotte. He didn't even want to blink for fear of missing something.

Glass cases on either side of the entrance displayed an array of wondrous and delectable items they would find on the menu, and an entire wall of shelves off to the left of the L-shaped room held bottles of specialized herb oils and wines. In the wall of the alcove stood a huge stone fireplace which roared an enthusiastic welcome to them as they were seated at a nearby table.

"Haven't seen you ladies in a while," the waiter said as he held out Lorette's chair. "What have you been up to? You haven't found yourselves another bistro, now have you?"

"Are you kidding?" Charlotte asked. "No one else makes shrimp and pasta like Evan. We wouldn't dare stray, you know that."

"She's been very busy." Lorette grinned at him over her shoulder. "You know James, but our other companion this evening is Seth Pruitt. Charlotte's new husband."

The man raised his sunbleached eyebrows and looked Seth over. He felt oddly like the next lobster for the pot.

"Well, you have indeed been busy then. Welcome to Char's favorite bistro, Mr. Pruitt. I expect we'll be seeing a great deal of you."

"Thank you," Seth replied, a cockeyed smile raised toward Charlotte.

"I get these cravings," she explained.

"You must get them quite often as well-known as you are here. Do they use you in their advertising?"

"Come and dine at Macaroni Grill," James said with a snort. "Where Charlotte Dennison comes to fulfill her cravings."

"The usual for four?" the waiter asked. "And a bottle of wine on the house to toast your marriage."

Seth noticed with amusement that the waiter didn't pause for a response. He was so sure that he knew their tastes, he simply decided what they would have and then headed off to order it up!

"Would it be too presumptuous to ask what the usual is?"

"You'll love it," Charlotte assured him with a pat to the top of his hand. "Broiled shrimp and fresh garlic with sauteed vegetables over angel hair pasta."

"Beginning with the best Caesar salad you've ever had," Lorette added. "Just wait and see. You'll love it."

Seth and James exchanged glances, and James shrugged his big shoulders and reached for the glass of water Chad, the waiter, set down in front of him.

"Here," Charlotte nudged Seth, and she pushed a tin of crayons across the table at him. "Dazzle me."

The invitation intrigued him. "I beg your pardon," he asked.

She picked up a green crayon from the bucket and began mapping out an intricate design of branches on the table in front of her.

"See?" she said, crinkling her nose up at him.

"They really do indulge her here, don't they?" he said, laughing.

"Everyone can do it," she replied. "All the tables have crayons."

"Now I see why she really comes here," he said, then began to poke through the various colors, pulling several out and setting them on the table.

As he began to mindlessly sketch on the paper tablecloth, Seth couldn't help stealing a look at Charlotte now and then. She was a paradox to him, he realized.

Light and easy, he repeated to himself for the thirtieth time since he'd left New York. *Easy does it. Don't rush in.*

"So, James," he began as he continued to doodle. "If that offer still holds for tomorrow, I'd like to take you up on it."

"You bet!"

"What offer?" Charlotte said as she looked up from what was becoming a crayon masterpiece.

"Seth has some experience with coaching," Lorette explained. "He's going over to practice with James tomorrow afternoon."

Charlotte's shot a glance at Seth, and he resisted the urge to laugh out loud at her reaction.

"How did you even know James coaches a youth baseball team?" she asked as she stared at Seth.

"We drove all the way out from the airport together yesterday," James exclaimed. "You don't think we had any conversation on the way?"

Charlotte pursed her lips and shot Lorette a funny smile. She could read her friend's mind, and she knew that this stab at sharing the bliss of domesticity was her little way of hammering yet one more nail into the coffin of Seth's dearly departed bachelorhood.

Oh, she's good, she thought with a grin. *Very, very good!*

"And we were thinking of a barbecue with the boys afterward," Lorette added. "You can make some of that potato salad you're so famous for."

Another good shot, Lorette, Charlotte brainwaved over to her. And somehow she was certain her friend would scrounge up a baby for Charlotte to cradle in her arms at some point during the outing as well.

"You're famous for your potato salad?" Seth inquired. "Yet another thing I don't know about you."

"Oh, yeah," she grinned as Chad filled their glasses with wine. "Pot lucks and picnics the world over have touted my potato salad as the best there is."

"I had no idea you were so Jane Wyatt."

"Just wait till you taste my brownies!"

Seth tossed the crayons down into the bucket and leaned back in his chair to take a long swig from his glass.

"Oh, Seth," Lorette cooed. "That is beautiful!"

They all looked down at the table where an elaborate drawing now filled the space of the once-blank tablecloth. Two hands clasped together bearing very familiar wedding rings were surrounded in an intricate ivy arch.

Beneath it, in perfect blocked letters, were the words that Charlotte read aloud.

"Set me as a seal upon thine heart, as a seal upon thine arm. For love is strong as death."

"What is that?" Lorette asked. "I know that verse."

"Song of Solomon," Seth told her, and she nodded.

"It's beautiful," Charlotte sighed, then looked up at Chad as he set four perfect salads on the table before them. "Could I get some scissors?"

When Chad nodded and headed off toward the kitchen, Charlotte smiled shyly at Seth, then down at the table.

"I want to keep it."

Since Charlotte had chosen the restaurant, James decided it was only fitting that he and Lorette decide on the entertainment after dinner. They drove out to Roswell to a little jazz bar set in the midst of a complex called The Mill, which housed a number of small shops and restaurants. They sipped Irish coffee, listened to music, and chatted for hours about everything from Seth's business pursuits to the tedium of working at Global to James's crazy Aunt Lucille.

Charlotte could see that Seth enjoyed her friends' company, and it made her feel even closer to him. She tried to ignore the occasional nod from Lorette that she could read like a page from a bold-typed novel, but she could clearly see the bond forming as well. Seth fit into her life as if the groove had already been molded to him long before they met. All he needed to do was settle into it.

The ride back to James and Lorette's was a cozy one, nestled side by side in the back seat, the fresh scent of the soft leather seats mixed with the spicy fragrance of Seth and the light floral of Charlotte. She closed her eyes and breathed in, dreaming to herself that their life together would always be reflected in the combination of sweet perfumes. Matched and perfectly suited to one another, neither one overpowering the other, just a melody of fragrance, one complementing the other.

Strains of Mozart whispered to them, and the world outside seemed far away as they sped through the night. She longed for Seth's strong arms to wrap around her, holding her so close to him that she could hear his heart beating over the hum of tires gliding along the smooth road. But he remained unbelievably casual.

"How about some wine?" Lorette asked when they reached the house, but Charlotte shook her head first, and Seth joined in agreement.

"We'll see you tomorrow," she said. "Thanks for such a great time tonight."

Lorette walked over to her, and the two friends embraced.

"Be happy," she whispered into Charlotte's ear. "He's fabulous."

"Yes. He is."

Charlotte handed over the keys to her Toyota and settled contentedly down into the passenger seat, though it was admittedly a far cry less inviting than the back of James's Lexus.

"Make a right on the main road and follow it straight out," she said, then raised up her knees beneath the full cotton skirt and planted her chin firmly upon them.

"They are good people," Seth told her as he tuned in the classical station they'd been listening to in James's car.

"Mmmm," she mumbled in agreement, then stretched, curled into a ball beside him on the seat, and took his hand into hers before closing her eyes.

"Don't go to sleep now," he warned her with a laugh. "We'll be halfway to Florida before we realize."

"I won't," she promised. "I'm just relaxing."

Charlotte couldn't remember feeling so completely sustained in all her life. She found herself wondering about the future, but she didn't dwell on the questions that haunted her mind like a distant melody. Things were too perfect just then to ruin them. The previous night had done nothing if not taught her a thing or two about timing!

She opened her eyes to find that they'd gone further than she'd thought.

"Make a left at the next light," she told him, then fell silent once more. She was leading him to her apartment over Mrs. Bernard's garage.

"You can drop me off and take the car to the hotel if you'd like," she said casually. "Then come back and get me in the morning."

He was silent for what seemed like an eternity. Then, at last, "Can I come in for a while?"

"Of course."

And her heart thankfully started beating again.

Chapter Twelve

"**A** glass of wine?" she asked him as he closed the door behind him.

"You know what I'd prefer? I've been dreaming about a cup of that special tea of yours for weeks."

She smiled, and it warmed him.

"I'll put the water on."

"You're going to feel like you've been paroled when you move into the other place," he told her as he looked around. "This is like a shoebox in comparison."

"I know," she said. "I don't know what I'll do when I get hungry in the middle of the night and have to take that long hike to the kitchen. Why, it will seem like an eternity!"

Their eyes met by accident, then held there for a long moment. He knew he had to speak up, and yet Seth felt immobilized under the heat of Charlotte's eyes. He approached her carefully, then stroked the side of her cheek with the gentle touch of two fingers. It was like the glide of a feather across satin.

"I think it's imperative that we enforce a strict rule of open communication," he told her as they sat down on the sofa, as if picking up some mysterious, unspoken conversation in mid-sentence.

"Good suggestion," she agreed, slipping her hand into his.

"I want to say right up front, Charlotte, that I think you are the most beautiful woman I've ever known."

The silence that followed was the loudest he'd ever encountered.

"What are you saying?" she finally asked him softly.

"I'm saying . . . let's get to know each other. Like . . . friends."

He wondered if it had sounded as bad to her as it did to him. Before she misunderstood, he continued.

"The Fourth of July comes once a year, Charlotte. And it's wonderful, with its excitement and fireworks and dramatic celebration. But there are three hundred sixty-four other days in every year. There are Christmases and Thanksgivings and rainy Sunday afternoons. I think it's important that we know each other on those days as well. Do you understand what I'm saying?"

She nodded thoughtfully, and it drew a smile on his face.

After Michele, Seth had pretty much given up on that dream of finding a woman who knew him inside out, who could finish his sentences and complete his thoughts. He had just resigned himself to the reality that he'd had his chance, and that one chance was gone. There was no such thing out there for him now, and he'd almost found peace with that resolution—until he got on a plane and sat down next to this woman who made him laugh, who touched him in a way that was nearly spiritual.

None of which he could bring himself to confess to her out loud at that moment, of course.

The whistle on the kettle screamed over them, but Charlotte didn't so much as flinch. The hazy, clouded fear that brimmed inside her probing hazel eyes seemed to hold her words prisoner.

"Let's just take this one step at a time," Seth whispered to her, and she silently nodded at him. He raised her chin toward him and planted a delicate kiss on her mouth. He could see straight inside her, she felt certain, and she closed her eyes to accept his sweet kiss.

Seth was too sensible to love impetuously, and Charlotte told herself she could learn something from his leisurely walk toward emotion.

The siren of the kettle droned on as he kissed her, but Charlotte hardly noticed.

Charlotte was in the kitchen in her pajamas, still chopping sweet pickles for the potato salad, when Seth arrived the next morning to pick her up. She recruited him to finish the job while she hurried into the tiny bathroom.

"I've been peeling and cooking for hours," she called to him as she ran the cold water over her hands and splashed her face.

"This looks like a meal in itself," he managed through a full mouthful. "And . . . it's . . . delicious."

"Wait until it's finished," she said with a laugh. "Stir them in when you're through chopping, will you?"

Seth didn't answer, and she imagined it was because he wasn't able to speak over the potato salad in his mouth! She listened carefully and heard the soft crunch of his nibbling, then shook her head and grinned.

"Seth!"

"I'm stirring, I'm stirring," he called back.

As she applied moisturizer to her face, Charlotte stepped over to the closet and pulled one of the pink hangers from inside. She hung the floral sundress on the outside of the door and hurried back into the bathroom. Where were those sandals, anyway?

She cast a quick glance at the bed as she passed. It looked as if someone had wrestled across it several times. The sheets were pulled away from the mattress, and the blanket was curled into a small ball at the corner. She hadn't slept well at all, and her bed betrayed her secret. Hurriedly, she straightened the bedclothes in a slightly haphazard way.

Despite the endless tossing and turning, she had arisen that morning with new resolve in regard to Seth. She planned to do everything she could to lull Seth Pruitt into the "ready" position. He wanted to see where they were headed, and she ached to show him what she was already sure of.

When she appeared in the doorway of the kitchen, she resisted the triumphant smile that jumped at Seth's reaction. He looked at her dreamily, as if he'd just spied a most beautiful vision.

The thick gathered straps of the dress fell perfectly across her slender shoulders, and the back of the dress was cut low, tipped with a bow that laced all the way up from her waist. Her hair was perfectly knotted at the top of her head, and a few feathery wisps still managed to cascade down the back of her neck and at the sides of her face.

"Have you finished the potato salad?" she asked, trying not to notice his reaction to her.

"Yes, dear," he said mockingly, and he stuck close as she moved about the tiny kitchenette, then stopped to watch her spoon the completed salad into a large wooden bowl.

"When are you moving from this cracker box anyway?"

he asked, dipping his finger in for one more taste before she playfully smacked it.

"I don't know," she admitted with the ticklish curl of her shoulder. "I have a full schedule. I don't know when I'll have the time."

"Let me take care of it for you," he said, and she turned to face him. "I know of this company that will come into your house, pack you up, move you, and unpack. All you have to do is come home to your new home at the end of your day."

"And how much do these wonderful little elves charge for such a service?"

"Think of it as my wedding gift," he said.

"I thought you were my wedding gift," she reminded him with a grin.

"Right. So let me handle it."

"Well, I can't let you do that."

"Why not?"

She looked at him seriously, both arms around the bowl of potato salad as she faced him.

"That's not the kind of thing you let someone do for you. I'll manage."

Her defiant gaze seemed to stop him in his tracks suddenly, and she smiled in hopes of putting him back at ease.

"So what's the name of this company of helpful little people?" she asked him as he locked the door and she headed down the stairs with the huge bowl.

"Weber's Move-You," he replied.

"Elves named Weber," she said. "I wouldn't have guessed."

Chapter Thirteen

Seth's first-of-the-month letter was much like the one that had come the month before. Doing fine, working on this project, making plans for that nuance of Fulton House, enclosed is payment in full. Charlotte read it over for the tenth or twelfth time before dropping it to the tabletop. How she had hoped . . .

She took a long look at the drawing Seth made on the tablecloth at Macaroni Grill, framed and matted as a wedding gift from Lorette, where it stood on the floor, leaning against the leg of the coffee table. Two clasped hands. She spat out an ironic chuckle. Their hands couldn't be further from clasped these days. They had reduced the art of taking it slow to a form all its own, a status just shy of stalled completely.

Charlotte had tried everything from subtle to obvious in the last month, anything and everything she could think of to get Seth's attention, to no avail. He had politely returned her phone calls at times when he knew good and well that she was at work, supplying her answering machine with curt little log lines about his life, much the same kind of thing she'd found in the letter which accompanied his check. So courteous and noncommittal that it made her want to scream. Or cry.

She had just about decided to put an end to her pain by calling off the whole deal with Seth until she'd gone by to visit her father earlier in the day. The manicured lawns and fresh scrubbed facilities of Heathcliffe had been enough to jolt that idea right from her head. She could never afford such a place without the assistance provided from Seth. And the alternatives she had found previously when hoping to cut costs left her as cold as his letter tossed haphazardly on the table.

She was stuck, and she knew it. She was as dependent on this so-called husband of hers as millions of other American wives who never had their spouses' time, attention, or affections. If she really thought about it, she fit right in now with the ranks of wives she'd vowed never to join. The hopelessness of the realization weighed her heavily down to the chair by the window.

"Seth," she whispered, never realizing how easily his name floated across her lips.

Things had looked so promising on his last visit. They'd fit together so perfectly, their lives amiably crossing over, their chemistry powerful at the very least. But once he'd left . . . He seemed to Charlotte to be gone in every sense of the word, and it confounded her.

Why couldn't she just enjoy the business relationship they'd been able to strike, she wondered. Why must it matter so much? Why couldn't she set Seth Pruitt in his rightful place just outside the fringes of her everyday life and move on?

The night was a shroud for Charlotte, a binding and constricting cloak that held no warmth or protection from the elements. Her mind raced in circles around memories and thoughts of Seth. By the time morning descended upon her, she had planned most of the details of the trek to New York that she was going to call spontaneous.

A shopping trip on a lark. A quick flight to see the Christmas decorations at Rockefeller Center, maybe. Oh, and how on earth could she visit The Big Apple and overlook Seth? Well, she just couldn't, that was all. Maybe they'd have time for dinner or a quick drink?

"One last shot," she vowed as she boarded the flight Thursday afternoon. If it worked out, great. If he was disinterested or, worse, actually rejected her, then she'd go home partially humiliated and partially resolved. At least she'd have given it one final stab either way.

Her Global ID entitled her to half-off on a room at The Plaza, and upon checking in, she immediately phoned Seth.

"Hello?"

She recognized that work-induced preoccupation right away, and she smiled as she ran a finger around the rim of the receiver. At least she'd reached him instead of his voice mail! She hadn't even considered that he might be out of town until her flight had already been underway, and she was relieved. Not only that he was in town, but at the mere sound of his familiar voice.

"Seth?"

"This is Seth Pruitt," he said impatiently. "Who's calling?"

"Mrs. Seth Pruitt," she replied playfully, a lilt of amusement dancing in her voice. "How soon they forget."

"Charlotte?"

And she could hear him slap the pen in his hand down to the desktop.

"Is something wrong?" he asked.

The brownstone where Seth lived surprised Charlotte. The neighborhood had an old-world kind of charm. Rows of buildings that looked pretty much the same were lined along a brick sidewalk, and most sets of stairs that led to the countless doors were lined with potted poinsettia plants wrapped in shiny tinfoil.

Holiday decorations abounded in themes of varied doctrines, from jolly Santas to lighted menorahs to simple crosses like the one that graced Seth's door.

Past the foyer loomed a huge living room set out upon a varnished oak floor partially covered in a rich Bokhara rug. The sofa was deep green leather, and a large wooden rocker sat to one side of the room. Several large windows with sills at knee-height dominated the far wall and stood two feet taller than Charlotte. They were covered in striking dark green window shades with deep golden tassels.

The key had been buried in the rock garden, just where Seth had promised, and she let herself in at his invitation to make herself at home until he was able to join her there.

Charlotte paused to inspect the countless framed photographs in the hallway. Each one depicted a different building, all of them of various styles and architecture. His finished products, she supposed, as she looked them over.

Charlotte entered the guest bedroom to the right and focused on the large brass bed. As she glanced around, she instinctively knew this was not Seth's suite. The walls of the room were paneled in rich oak slats, except for one wall which was papered in a deep blue paisley design.

The bedspread matched the wall in hue and was set off by a large burgandy settee positioned near the window. A tall wooden armoire stood elegantly against one wall, and large slatted oak doors folded open to reveal a lighted walk-in closet.

As she made her way down the hall, Charlotte grinned

at the sudden fantasy of following Seth around his apartment. How she longed to belong there, and how that realization frightened her all of a sudden!

A king-sized four-poster bed dominated the room at the end of the hallway, and a bureau in the corner displayed several framed photographs, including a copy of the wedding picture Dyann had taken. Charlotte picked up the carved wooden frame and looked closely before smiling, then setting it back into place. She could easily see Seth living much of his life in this room, and she ran a hand along the back of the chair placed at the writing desk situated diagonally in the corner.

She glanced around cautiously then, like a child aware of the possibility of being discovered rifling through someone else's personal items. She then flinched at the very thought.

Charlotte moved carefully to the bed and looked over it. The pillows had been fluffed clean of the indentation she knew his head made the night before. She ran her palm gently across the case, then snatched the pillow from its resting place and hugged it to her chest, inhaling the familiar scent of him as deeply in as she could manage.

"Charlotte?"

His voice cut through her, and she threw the pillow back to its place in sheer panic. He couldn't find her in there! Not in his bedroom, of all places. He'd know she'd been snooping. He'd know all sorts of things!

"Please, God," she prayed as she hurried out into the hall and made a quick left through swinging oak doors just as she spotted his coatsleeve making a turn to the hall from the living room.

"Charlotte?"

The kitchen was fit for a gourmet, and Charlotte scanned every direction for an alibi.

"In here," she finally called, snatching a glass from the dishrack in the sink. "In the kitchen."

"Seth," she said nonchalantly as he stepped into the room. "I was just getting a drink of water."

"Have you been waiting long?" he asked, and she shook her head casually as she ran water into the glass and took a long drink.

"You're a sight," he said, facing her.

"You, too."

And he was indeed!

Seth was beyond handsome. She sometimes forgot just how so—the way the light seemed to shine in his crystal eyes, the way a room ignited at the spark of his contagious smile. Charlotte found herself returning the rays of his broad grin without even intending to do so.

He seemed apprehensive at first as he opened his arms to her, like a high school senior greeting his date for the prom.

Okay, she thought, this is why I'm here! To test the waters of opportunity.

Charlotte moved into those open arms and settled in as if she'd come home after a long journey. There was a slight rock to their embrace, a shared rhythm that each of them knew instinctively.

With her eyes closed tight, her arms wrapped around his muscular torso, her head nuzzled beneath his chin, Charlotte sighed.

She hated herself for the emotion that raced through her at his touch, and she wondered if her pounding heart had betrayed her completely.

"Would you like a tour?" he asked, and she nodded, relieved that his polite question hadn't required her to grab deep for her voice.

Seth led her back into the hallway, where she had narrowly escaped discovery, and she viewed both bedrooms with feigned first-time interest. Down the short hall and to the end, they crossed over to a door which led to Seth's office.

In the corner, an antique drafting table overlooked the street through a shuttered window, while the opposite wall was flanked by a large oak desk and several tall wooden file cabinets. Seth pulled the chain on the green-shaded brass lamp, and yellowish light flooded the desktop.

"Would you like to see the plans for Fulton House?"

"I'd love to," she exclaimed, then plopped down in the large brown leather chair and spun around several times. "I saw the photos in there of your other projects. Soon Fulton House will be hanging right there in the hall with the others!"

"Oh, Seth," she said as she perused the drawings and sketches he presented.

Fulton House was Seth's baby, the project he had been longing to complete. A five-star bed and breakfast going up on the west side that, if all went according to plan, the financers had agreed to back in eleven more cities across the United States. This exclusive inn was the opportunity Seth had been dreaming about since he was a fledgling architect striking out on his own. It was the culmination of all of his hopes and plans, and Fulton House would set his plan at least two years ahead of schedule.

The building was Victorian in architecture, yet more elegant than ornate. The simple floral landscaping in the sketch seemed to be as much a part of the overall design as the partial-brick face or arched bay window.

"Seth, it's so beautiful," she told him. "You really are so talented."

When the doorbell rang, Charlotte lagged behind in order

to place the sketches neatly back into their files, and she entered the living room just in time to greet the friendly stranger who seemed very much at home there.

"Is this her?" he asked with a perfect, white smile.

"This is her."

She sensed a distant pang of discomfort in Seth's usual composure.

"So," he said as he approached her, his hand outstretched, "you're the one who's stolen him."

"I beg your pardon?"

"Peter and I have had a standing agreement," Seth began, but Peter interrupted with a good-natured smack to his friend's back.

"No wives, no distractions," he sang like a familiar chant. "I keep hoping he'll get fat from the lack of exercise, but so far you seem to be keeping him quite fit."

Color rose over Charlotte's face, and she smiled politely.

If something's keeping Seth fit, she thought, *it certainly isn't me.*

"My racquetball partner," Seth explained with a wholehearted laugh, "refuses to believe I might become some sort of moderate success and not have time for him. So he insists on blaming you."

"Not you, per se," he said to her. "But the unholy state of wedded bliss we'd always vowed to avoid together. My sizeable ego simply can't face being rolled over in the name of business, but seeing this work of art," he said as he waved his hand before her like a magic wand, "makes it far less of a dispute."

"Getting thick in here," Seth said, and Charlotte couldn't help but giggle.

"Now that you're here," Peter continued, "perhaps we can share him for a couple of hours Friday morning." Then, glancing at Seth, he added, "She might enjoy working out at the club."

Charlotte shot a questioning look at Seth.

"There's a heated pool and a sauna," Peter went on. "All the amenities. We could make a morning of it."

"She's only going to be here for such a short time," Seth said, but Charlotte's interest was piqued.

"It sounds like fun," she said, and Seth slowly agreed with a shrug that left Charlotte cold.

What is he thinking?

"Nine o'clock out front," Peter said victoriously. "I'll leave you two to your spousal duties then. Good to finally meet you, Charlotte."

"You, too, Peter."

He was a good-looking man, she noted as he sauntered out the door. His black hair was thick and wavy, and his deep brown eyes were caped in luxurious dark lashes.

"He lives two doors down," Seth said. "He can be a little pushy, but he's a good guy."

"I liked him," she replied. "It will be fun."

"Are you hungry?" he asked. "We could go out, or I can throw something together here. I think I have a couple of steaks . . . Uh, unless you have other plans?"

"No. I can make a salad," she said. "Do you have the greens?"

"Some," he told her. "Let's check the fridge."

Seth poured them glasses of club soda while they both set about their own duties in the kitchen. The room was big enough for two couples to cook dinner, Charlotte thought, and she expected they might never even run into each other!

"So tell me," she began as she stood across the butcher block island from him, chopping cucumbers for the salad.

"When does the actual construction begin on Fulton House?"

"We're looking at the last week in April," he replied. "Assuming the winter is short."

"Please, God, let the winter be short," she playfully directed upward.

"Amen," Seth added with a mock-serious expression. "We have a whole group of really talented people in on this project. They're having a cocktail party out at Windom's tomorrow night if you're interested in meeting them and playing the part of the new little wife? I think they've all been wondering why I haven't brought you around."

The new little wife.

The words sprang up within her.

She hadn't brought anything to wear that was appropriate for her first cocktail party as Mrs. Seth Pruitt, but she could do some of that shopping she'd hoped to do in the city the following afternoon. Her mind was suddenly jumping like a subway car on an automatic track.

"It might be a very good business move, actually." He seemed to be thinking out loud. "If you're game, anyway."

His offhanded attitude toward their domestic bliss didn't go unnoticed, but she tried hard not to dwell on it. If he wanted to parade her around as a business opportunity, a wife, or wear her as a cuff link for heaven's sake, she didn't care. Just being with him was worth capitalizing on for the moment.

Proximity.

That's what Lorette had cited as their greatest disadvantage. An adversary worth conquering, she had decided in making this trip. And conquer it, she would!

"It's the least I can do," she said casually. "After all, you did the same for me."

Chapter Fourteen

The taupe suit she'd found in Manhattan was elegant, and she had to admit that she'd never spent so much on one outfit in her entire life, but she was able to justify it.

The skirt was form-fitting and slit several inches up the back, and the matching collarless jacket was just three inches shorter than the skirt itself. It was set off by beautiful neutral beading on the front, carried down in a spray upon full chiffon sleeves.

Anyone would have thought the shoes had been dyed to match, so perfectly coordinated were they to the suit, and light nylon stockings shimmered slightly against the skin of her long, shapely legs. She hadn't been to the gym in months, she recalled as she examined her reflection in the full-length mirror, and she hoped that Seth's club had a Stairmaster she could use to recommit to her former fitness regimen before the signs of neglect began to manifest.

Not that Charlotte was a physique fanatic, of course. But

she did have heightened resolve to make herself as attractive for Seth as she possibly could, the same way she wanted to improve upon every other area as well. She now wanted to become a better housekeeper, maybe take a gourmet cooking class.

Domesticity is an organism that spreads, she thought, *to every corner of your life when you fall in love. Perhaps someone should take it upon themselves to issue a warning, like the one on the side of cigarette packs.*

A knock at her hotel room door startled her and set her heart frantically pounding.

"Come in for a moment," she invited Seth with a smile, and she tried to ignore how perfect he looked as she finished up her tasks. "I'm almost ready."

She hurried to the bed and transferred several items from her large leather bag to the small evening purse she'd purchased for the occasion. Some cash, the tester tube of Jessica McClintock perfume, a package of breath mints. She paused at the mirror to paint a rich frosty glaze to her lips with a gold brush before dropping it into the purse as well.

Seth was a vision to her, and she swallowed hard beneath the weight of his smile. In a white dinner jacket, black trousers, and bow tie, he looked like something atop a wedding cake, and she stifled the urge to place him there in her imagination, even for a moment.

The long black coat she'd brought went fine with all of the casual things she'd packed, but it seemed dowdy over such a sophisticated ensemble. She made a mental note to slip out of it the moment they stepped inside the front door of the Windom home.

Charlotte didn't know what she expected as they drove out to Long Island but, whatever it was, the reality of the Windom home wasn't it.

It couldn't even be called a house, not with a straight

face anyway. It was more a mansion, set right on the water's edge, a small marina of yachts rocking gently in its backdrop. Visions of a small cocktail party at the tasteful home of Seth's associates sailed right out the window as they pulled up into the circular drive and were met by a valet offering to park Seth's Ford Probe for them. Charlotte fought the urge to shed her coat right there and make the trek to the door in the freezing cold.

"Don't be silly," Seth said. "No one will even notice."

If the gentleman at the door who relieved them of their coats did notice, he didn't let on, and she felt suddenly transformed the moment the ragged thing was out of her sight. She was amused by the momentary vision of its return at the end of the evening. If anyone was there to witness it, she would simply vehemently deny its ownership and opt instead to make off with another guest's mink.

"Seth, my boy!" someone called, and Charlotte turned to see a man heading toward them. He was refined and perfectly tailored in what she guessed was at least a $1,500 suit. His silver hair glistened, and when he smiled the moustache of the same silver hue smiled along with him.

"Clayton, how are you?"

"It's a festive evening," the gentleman announced, then clapped Seth gently on the back.

"I'd like you to meet my wife," Seth stated so matter-of-factly that it left a tiny echo in the pit of Charlotte's stomach. "Clayton Windom, Charlotte Dennison-Pruitt."

Her name seemed to sing as he spoke it, and Charlotte decided right there and then to officially take it. Charlotte Dennison-Pruitt. She might like to be hyphenated, after all.

"Mr. Windom, it's a pleasure," she said, beaming. "Seth has told me such wonderful things about you and the Fulton House project."

"So you are the mysterious wife," he said, sizing her up.

Politely, of course, but she could not mistake the intention. "He goes off on a quick weekend to the wedding of a friend, and he comes back a married man," he continued. "I must admit that we all wondered if you really did exist or if the name of Charlotte was just the concoction of a confirmed bachelor trying to remain that way."

"I warned you that she was real," Seth said with a laugh.

"She's the replica of an angel," Windom replied. "Charlotte, dear, welcome to my home."

"Thank you for having me." She tried to smile, but there was something about the way he'd looked her over that stuck with her, and Charlotte wasn't entirely sure that she liked the man.

"Introduce your lovely wife to Angelica," he said, and it seemed more like a command than an invitation. "The buffet is first-rate and the liquor is flowing freely. Have yourselves a pleasant evening."

"Thank you, Clay," Seth acknowledged, then slipped his hand around Charlotte's with a squeeze.

"Why do I get the feeling I've trespassed?" she whispered as they made their way into the bustling room, but Seth responded with nothing more than a light chuckle.

"Who's Angelica?"

The woman emerged from the crowd as if on cue, and Charlotte instantly knew who she was.

"Seth Pruitt," she cooed as she took his hand and coiled hers around it like a snake. "Why didn't you tell us you were going to be bringing your little wife along? This is she, isn't it? You are Charlene, aren't you?"

"Charlotte." She forced a polite smile. *The little wife?*

"Oh, Charlotte. That's right. Seth, darling, have you spoken to Navotny yet?"

"He's here?"

"Yes. His wife's name is Devin. You won't be able to miss her. She's the large cowlike woman in the polka-dots."

Charlotte turned something invisible and sour over in her mouth. What a distasteful woman this Angelica was. Oh, she was beautiful, all right. Her bleached-golden hair fell halfway down her back in teased and sprayed spiral curls, and the porcelain nails she'd painted red to match her gown must have cost a fortune to maintain. Charlotte didn't like her one bit.

What she mostly didn't like about her, far above and beyond the criticism of others and her high-and-mighty air, was the way she still held on to Seth's hand relentlessly, and the feathery way she kept calling him "darling."

"Darling, you must pay a visit to the buffet. The crab soufflé is marvelous. Go on," she cooed, waving those fingernails in his face and finally releasing his ravaged hand. "Make yourself a plate and give me a moment to get acquainted with your new little wife."

Seth shot a look at her, and Charlotte knew with just one panicked glance from her he would refuse, make excuses, and rescue her from Angelica's clutches. But she had to show him that she could stand on her own in situations like this—that she could be the sort of wife who fought her own battles and drew her own territorial lines without sitting back and waiting on her husband to hoist out his sword and do battle on her behalf. She had always believed that kind of wife was tiring, and she wanted to start things off right. She was sure that tonight they were embarking upon their official beginning.

Following a barely perceptible nod from Charlotte, Seth set out toward the enormous array of food displayed on the tables in front of the rock fireplace in the adjoining dining room. He was held up several times on his way, and she noticed that he kept looking back at her over the shoulders of chatty acquaintances. Willing to throw the lifeline at any given moment, she supposed.

"So, tell me, Charlene," Angelica began, and Charlotte decided not to correct her. "What do you do exactly? Are you an artist of some kind like our Seth?"

My Seth, Charlotte corrected in her mind. And she would hardly limit Seth's abilities as an architect to a term so broad as "artist."

"I work for Global Airlines," she explained, swallowing the resentment of her asking.

"Oh, a travel agent?"

"I'm in Reservations," she explained, and Angelica's glazed look told her that the woman couldn't have cared less had she admitted to servicing the planes.

"And how did you and our Seth meet?" she asked. "He's been so mysterious about you ever since he told us you'd been married."

"On a Global flight, actually," she replied.

"Love at first sight, I suppose. And who can blame you. Seth is quite the exquisite young man."

"Yes, he is. In the three short hours from Atlanta to Las Vegas, I knew I'd never shake the effects of meeting him." She took enormous pleasure in the secret amusement of the double meaning.

"Tell me," she began, but Angelica was interrupted as someone called her name and appeared at her side.

"How are you, Phoebe? So glad you could make it this evening."

"Excuse me." Charlotte grabbed hold of the first opportunity of escape and executed it masterfully.

She'd lost sight of Seth and made her way to the bar for a glass of Chardonnay to hold on to for the rest of the evening. She moved from room to room and finally spotted

Seth on a brocade upholstered couch in deep conversation with a group of three other men. Charlotte hoped they wouldn't be staying long.

"Charlotte," Seth called, and she moved to his side. "Gentlemen, this is my wife. Charlotte, meet Edward Barnes, Terry Noble, and Jack MacGregor. Various attorneys and representatives of Windom Industries on the Fulton House project."

"Glad to meet you," she replied sweetly as she perched on the arm of the couch beside Seth.

"We've been looking forward to meeting the elusive Mrs. Pruitt," MacGregor said.

"That seems to be the sentiment of the evening," she replied.

"All right, Mac," Seth warned good-naturedly. "That's enough."

"Don't worry, Pruitt, old boy. I'm not planning to embarrass you."

Charlotte wondered what he meant by that, but decided to let it pass until a more appropriate time presented itself to ask.

"We were just discussing the preliminary plans for the Fulton franchise," Seth told her. "Terry has the idea that we might go worldwide rather than national."

"I think American travelers abroad would appreciate a name they recognize," Nolan explained. "A classy and comfortable room from a name they know they can count on, only flavored with the local color of that particular city. The dinner menu is always regional, reflecting the tastes of the culture."

"Breakfast, on the other hand," Mac added, "is your generic American fare with some color thrown in."

"What cities do you have in mind?" she asked.

"Paris, of course," Barnes answered. "London. Madrid."

"Tokyo would be good," said Nolan. "I have to go to Tokyo a lot on business."

"And he wants a free place to stay," Mac teased, and they all chuckled lightheartedly at Nolan's expense.

"The actual decor will be Angelica's territory," Barnes explained. "But the design of each house stems directly from the brillance of your husband's imagination."

"See, honey," she directed at Seth. "I'm not the only one who recognizes your brillance. You mentioned Angelica choosing the decor. I wasn't aware. Is she involved in the project?"

"You haven't told your wife about Angelica, eh?" Mac asked. "Very strategic move, buddy. Only now we've blown it for you."

"Angelica is an interior designer," Seth explained. "And she's the bulk of the money behind Fulton House.

"She and your husband work together. *Very* closely," MacGregor emphasized, and she wanted to slap him. "Until well into the night on some occasions, huh, Pruitt?"

"Do your worst, Mac," Seth replied. "If this is the only way you can get your kicks, press on. Go ahead. Charlotte is well aware that she is the only woman in the world I have any desire to be with, aren't you, darling?"

"I believe I am, sweetheart," she answered, jumping right in.

"You two deserve each other," MacGregor said, belly-laughing.

"Did you hear that, honey?" Seth exclaimed as he rose from his chair and wrapped his arm tightly around Charlotte's waist. "The MacGregor stamp of approval is on our marriage. What more could we ever want? Freshen your wine, dear?"

"Please."

And the two of them walked away in triumph.

"What a wonderful team we make," Seth whispered, then Charlotte leaned in closer.

"How far into the night do you and Angelica work, anyway?"

"Not far," he said with a peck to her cheek. "Not far at all."

Chapter Fifteen

Seth tugged unconsciously at the tie binding his throat as he watched Charlotte glide about the room. She seemed to float on a breeze, effortlessly mesmerizing everyone around her, man or woman, attached or single.

He couldn't make out the words, but he watched intently as she delicately placed a selection of snacks on the china plate balanced on her hand, expertly dodging the obvious flirtations of Jack MacGregor all the while. Seth darted his gaze away when she glanced at him, and the crackle of shared laughter between her and Mac drew it directly back like some unavoidable magnetic force of nature.

He'd made such excellent use of the time that had passed since he'd left Atlanta—and Charlotte—behind him. He'd returned to his life in New York, vowing not to come into contact with Charlotte again until he could follow his own advice and move ahead slowly. Cautiously.

He'd nearly exorcised the final traces of her perfume

from his nostrils, the memory of the silken skin of her face, and the unforgettable light in her hazel eyes. Charlotte Dennison had become a magical lost dream, the crash of an ocean wave or the ringing of church bells far in the distance. Until he'd picked up the phone and heard her voice. Until he came home to find her standing carelessly in his kitchen without a trouble in the world, her face caressably inviting, her smile so lovely.

He grinned as he remembered the way his heart had begun to pound at her simple embrace. He had wondered if she'd been able to feel it beating against her. If she did, she never let on.

"Pruitt, what have you done in your life to deserve such a treasure?"

Seth jumped when he realized Clayton Windom was suddenly at his side, staring wistfully in Charlotte's direction.

"I was just wondering that very thing," he replied honestly.

"It's a rare thing when a woman brings about the kind of love I see in your eyes. Such a woman should be cherished. I hope you plan to do that, Seth."

"Yes, sir," he said, and the two of them shared a long look before Windom turned and stepped away to join a conversation already in progress.

A slight pinch tugged at Seth's chest, and Charlotte's laughter drew his attention back toward her. He eyed every detail of her across the room, from the muscular lines of her long, shapely legs to the arch of her brows as she listened attentively to one of Mac's endless tales.

No woman had ever touched him the way Charlotte had. And having her there inside his world stirred him. Seth had never wanted or needed a wife, and yet there she was. His wife.

* * *

"You were fantastic tonight," Seth told her in the car on the drive home. "I was so proud."

"Do you mean that?" Her heart stopped, waiting for his confirmation.

"Of course I do!"

"Seth . . ." She didn't know if she was hedging because she didn't want to ask the question, or perhaps because she didn't want to hear the answer. "Were you and Angelica involved?"

He was silent for a long moment before replying. "Briefly."

"What would possess you to date a woman like her?"

"We were working very closely together," he explained. "This was before you and I met. And one dinner led to another, one late night to another late night, and I found myself—"

"In her clutches," she finished for him.

"Charlotte, I meant it when I said it was brief. You could hardly call it a relationship. Just a few dates, with no real meaning at all. I ended things between us weeks before I even met you."

"Funny," she replied thoughtfully. "I don't think it's over for Angelica."

"Don't be ridiculous," he countered. "Angelica Windom can land just about any man she sets her sights on. What does she need with a seemingly happily married man when there are so many other fish out there to fry?"

"Windom?" she repeated, then turned sideways in the seat to face him. "She's Windom's . . ."

"Daughter," he said. "Yes."

"Seth, I don't mean any offense, but are you crazy? Getting involved with the woman who holds the financial reins to your entire future? What could you have been thinking?"

"I'm not proud of it, Charlotte," Seth replied. "But in

the beginning, I don't suppose I was thinking at all. She's a very beautiful woman, and she was pursuing me. I wasn't in a relationship with anyone else."

"How did she take it when you broke it off with her?"

"Like a woman with other options," he said. "We agreed that the workplace was nowhere to enter into something personal. It was never serious between us."

Charlotte had sensed Angelica's intention to corner her all evening, and now she felt certain she knew what Angelica had on her bleached-blond mind. Although the exact words weren't there, the sentiment was all too clear. With a shudder, she reached over and cranked up the heater a couple of notches.

"Are you chilly?" Seth asked her, then extended his arm to pull her close into him.

"Yes," she said. "I'm suddenly very cold."

Charlotte had hoped Seth would invite her back to his brownstone, but he'd driven directly into town and to The Plaza.

"Come up for a drink?" she asked casually as they headed across the elegant lobby, and Seth nodded just as casually in silent agreement.

She thought she felt a spark of electricity pass between them when their eyes met for a brief eternity in the elevator, then convinced herself she was mistaken as he politely held the door for her like any gentleman as they walked into her room.

"I'll call down for hot water," she said, heading directly for the phone. "Vanilla almond tea?"

"Sounds perfect."

She watched him slip out of his dinner jacket and place it carefully over the back of the chair at the desk.

"Hungry?" she asked, then grinned as he shook his head.

"Could I have a pot of hot water for two, and some cream, sent up to Room 1614, please? Thank you."

She felt alarmingly like a high school student trapped in a hotel room with her dreamy professor as she sank to the edge of the bed and nervously smoothed the corner of the comforter.

"You look lovely, Charlotte," Seth commented, and she didn't dare look up at him.

"Thank you."

It wasn't until she felt him sit down on the bed beside her that she raised her hazel eyes.

"Like a bride again," he said with a smile, and she returned it shyly.

"I think I'm overdressed for a wedding." She giggled. "At least, if ours was any indication."

"I don't think our ceremony was any indication of any other," he returned, and the two of them shared a chuckle.

Only a moment later, Seth touched his hand to the side of Charlotte's face, and the two of them fell silent and serious as their eyes rested on each other.

"Charlotte," he whispered, and her heart began to race at the mere sound of her name passing across his full, inviting lips. Sometimes it was like a moment frozen in time for her, hearing him speak her name, and she had to just stop and listen to it.

He placed his arm around her and pulled her close to him.

"I'm so glad you came to New York," he whispered, and relief flowed through her entire body.

"I wasn't sure," she began, then fell silent for a long moment. "I guess I wanted to see if you were missing me the way I've been missing you."

"You've missed me?" he teased, and she chuckled.

"That is a pathetic and shameless attempt to solicit an ego-builder, Pruitt. I'm very disappointed in you."

The sun had barely risen when the two of them stepped through the front door into Seth's brownstone, Charlotte's bags in tow, each of them wrapped around the other like twine around a Christmas parcel, grinning and exchanging an easy conversation about the holidays of their youth.

"I'll put the water on for tea," Charlotte declared as they separated.

"And I'll put your bags in the guest room."

A surge of excitement rushed through her as she held the kettle beneath the faucet and looked around Seth's kitchen. She came to New York on a lark, a final shot at winning him over, and she had succeeded beyond her wildest imaginations. The blood inside her body coursed through with one idea about the future after another. One question followed the other, and before she knew it the kettle had overflowed and she had to pour out the excess.

Seth deposited Charlotte's bags near the ottoman in the corner, and he curiously noted his glowing smile in the reflection of the mirror above the dresser.

Why was he smiling so incessantly? Then it came to him.

This woman in his kitchen—with the hazel eyes and a thick mane of silky hair, with a smile of sensuality, innocence, and trust—this woman was *his wife*.

When she finally returned to the living room with two cups of brewed tea, Seth was stretched out on the sofa, sketches and blueprints around him and on the floor at his feet.

"Don't tell me," she said as she nestled into the tiny blank spot left beside him, "let me guess. Fulton House."

He returned the smile with a shrug. "It's everything, Charlotte. It's what I've worked my whole life for. There hasn't been a day in the last ten years that I haven't thought of it, strived toward it, prayed for it. Even when it didn't have a name, it was still a dream off in the distance. And now . . ."

Seth leaned into her, resting the back of his head against her arm and staring thoughtfully into the lights on the tree. The room had grown dark despite the hour as a snowstorm brewed outside. Charcoal clouds floated aimlessly across a blackened sky, and the wind made a whistling sound as it passed by the large panes of glass.

"All those dreams of yours are about to come true," she told him, smoothing his hair away from his eyes.

"But Fulton House isn't the only dream coming true for me this Christmas."

"It's not?" she asked hopefully.

"We have something very special, Charlotte. I'd given up on finding someone to grow old with. Someone I'd want to grow old with."

"And you've found someone like that?"

"Now who's the one extracting an ego boost?" he teased, then grew serious again. "Not only do I want to grow old with you, Charlotte. But I can't imagine growing old *without* you."

"Oh, Seth."

"I love you," he said after a silent moment.

"I love you, too," she replied, smoothing back his hair and caressing his temples tenderly.

Each of them remained silent except for their quiet breathing, which purred harmoniously, completely in sync. For nearly an hour, they sat there, cuddling one another, the only conversation whispered declarations of love muttered occasionally into the dark room illuminated only by the tiny white lights of the holiday tree.

* * *

The Stairmaster wasn't the workout Charlotte remembered. Either someone had turned the intensity switch up to a 10 or she had deteriorated in terms of endurance.

In less than fifteen minutes, she was ready to keel over. She tried momentarily to blame it on the upper body machines she had used previously, but laughed at herself and shook her head as she pressed on. She was happy that Peter had railroaded Seth to the racquetball court. She wouldn't have wanted him to see this!

Just five more minutes, she decided. *If I can live through five more minutes, I'll go sit in the sauna.*

"You're a better woman than I am," someone said behind, her. She paused to look over her shoulder and found Angelica leaning in the doorway.

Yes, I am. So what's your point?

"You're in far better shape than you look, dear. How long have you been at that thing?" Angelica went on.

"I don't know," Charlotte panted as the lie formed on the tip of her tongue. "Half an hour, I suppose."

The pink and gray workout leotard Seth had chosen for her in the club shop suddenly seemed tight, and she felt certain she was bulging in all the wrong places as Angelica climbed aboard the machine across from her.

The woman was a living ad for *Bodies of Steel.* Her revealing black leotard revealed that her body was virtually flawless. Charlotte tried not to stare, but she was itching to catch a glimpse of Angelica to see if she broke out into a sweat.

Five more minutes and Charlotte could envision a stroke on her horizon, so she warmed down for just another minute before stepping off.

"Oh, you're through?" Angelica asked, narrowing her eyes like a cat.

"Yes. I thought I'd take a sauna before grabbing a shower."

"A sauna. Now that sounds heavenly. May I join you?"

Rats!

"Of course, but don't let me break your stride. I'll grab a bottle of water and meet you in there."

The last thing on earth Charlotte wanted to do was get naked in front of Angelica Windom! But she sat down on the bench by the far wall inside the sauna, scantily wrapped in a terrycloth towel. She dipped a sponge into the bowl of water, wringing it out on her neck. The water was luke-warm, but it felt good as it drizzled down the length of her torso. She was just taking her first drink from the bottle of cold Evian when Angelica stepped inside.

"That must have been quite a workout, from the looks of you," she noted. "Are you all right?"

"Fine," Charlotte replied, clenching her teeth.

"I take it our Seth is here with you today?"

My Seth.

"Yes."

"On the racquetball court, no doubt," Angelica said as she stretched out longways on the bench across from Char-lotte, bending her slender leg, and leaning up on her elbow like a magazine ad. "He used to have a standing appoint-ment every Friday morning."

"With Peter. Yes, I know."

It felt good to flaunt a little of her own knowledge of her husband.

I'm not just the new kid on the block.

"Peter. An English professor, isn't he?"

Score one for the witch. "I'm not sure," she had to admit, and it just about killed her. "I can't remember."

The steam seemed to get thick in Charlotte's lungs, and she couldn't breathe very well. She sat up very straight and took a long swig from the bottle of water. Was it the steam that she thought she could cut with a knife, or was it just the tense atmosphere?

"Tell me, Charlene—"

"Charlotte," she interrupted softly. "My name is Charlotte."

"Oh, of course. Charlotte. Tell me, Char-lotte," she said. "What's up with you and Seth, anyway?"

"What do you mean?"

"I mean, no one ever hears of you. Not even a mention. And then suddenly, out of nowhere, he marries you. I know Seth just about as well as any woman can know a man— I assume he told you that we were involved?"

"Yes. He mentioned that."

I could strangle her, yes. But where would I hide the body?

"Well, I'm sure I know Seth better than just about anyone, and I can't imagine him doing something so impetuous."

"And yet, he did."

"What's the secret, Charlotte? What would make him do something so out of character?"

"The course of true love is often unpredictable," Charlotte said as she tried to smile, then shrugged her shoulders and took another swig of cool water.

"I don't think so."

Angelica pulled herself upright to face Charlotte squarely. "In my experience, love has a much different face than the one Seth was wearing when he announced his marriage."

"No offense intended, *Angela*," she began, then paused, waiting for the witch to correct her. But Angelica just glared at her, so Charlotte continued. "I don't really think the intimate details of our lives are any of your concern."

"You know, *Char-lene*, that's not exactly true. Anything Seth does is my concern."

"And how do you come to that conclusion?"

"I hold the cards," she said with a sneer. "There is something Seth wants more than anything in this life, dear heart. Even more than he wants *you*."

Charlotte didn't need to hear more. She already knew.

"Fulton House," the witch told her. "I can play the cards out to the end. Or not."

"What does that mean, exactly?" she asked, folding her hands neatly in her lap so that Angelica wouldn't notice the trembling.

"It means . . . I want you to leave Seth, Charlotte."

Charlotte stared at her for several long moments, waiting. A twitch at the corner of her mouth ached to curl into a smile. She had to be joking. Didn't she?

"Who do you think you are?" Charlotte said slowly, deliberately.

"I think I'm the person with the key to Seth's future," Angelica stated, maddeningly calm as she doused herself with water with the nearby sponge. "I can either fulfill all the things he's dreaming of, or I can yank it away in the blink of an eye."

"You really are a very sick person."

"Sick. No," she said candidly. "Powerful and fully aware how to use that power to my best advantage? Yes."

"Seth was never serious about you to begin with," Charlotte said, and she found herself trying to reason with the witch, despite knowing there was no real point. "Even if I packed up and left him this afternoon, he wouldn't turn to you."

"Don't be so sure," she returned. "We were a powerful force together."

"That's the second time you've used that word," Charlotte pointed out. "Power is a very important thing to you, isn't it?"

"When placed in the right hands, power is the only thing. But I'm not surprised you don't have the good sense to know that."

Charlotte narrowed her eyes, and Angelica shrugged arrogantly.

"Let me exercise that power for you, Charlotte, by pointing out the obvious. Number one, money makes the world go 'round. Number two, I am the money behind Fulton House. Number three, the secondary backer just happens to be my father, who adores me. Do you know the kind of loyalty that exists between a father and a daughter?"

Charlotte couldn't reply. Her father had been gone—absent really—for so long.

"You would really take a loss of the hundreds of thousands of dollars you've already invested in Fulton House?" Charlotte asked, hoping to wreak even the most minuscule crack in the witch's armor. "Over a man who doesn't even love you? Who never loved you?"

"A mere tax credit," she replied. "I have it to lose. Seth doesn't. If he loses Fulton House, he loses everything. He starts from scratch. Are you willing to do that to him?"

Nausea rose up inside her, and she wanted desperately to run. To go and grab Seth off the court and tell him everything the witch was saying, reveal every vile suggestion she'd made. But she didn't run out. She sat there, as if someone had glued her to the bench.

And indeed someone had.

Angelica Windom held the gluebrush, and Charlotte was utterly powerless before her, which was what the witch had no doubt planned all along.

Chapter Sixteen

"Well, Charlotte?" Angelica prodded. "Are you willing to destroy him like that?"

"You're the one destroying him, not me."

"No," she corrected, pointing one of those sharp red fingernails at Charlotte from across the sauna. "You have the power in your hands to ensure that Seth has everything he ever dreamed of."

"Except me."

"I think you and I both know you are not the woman Seth has always dreamed of, Charlotte. There's something beneath this marriage, something that holds it up. But his love and devotion to you aren't it. And besides, even if they were, Seth would get over you. It may take some time, some distance, but he will forget you. Losing Fulton House? Now there's something he would never forget."

Charlotte knew that she was right. But she refused to breathe even a hint of agreement.

"If you tell Seth about this little talk we've had, Charlotte," she said as she rose to her feet, "or if he comes to the progress meeting tomorrow afternoon without the sad news of your breakup, I will pull the plug on the Fulton House project. And our Seth will watch his dream go spinning into space. All because of you."

Charlotte watched her go, but couldn't summon the energy, or inspiration, to speak. She blinked her eyes. This was just a horrible nightmare, she told herself.

Wake up! Just wake up and everything will be fine.

The ride home was silent aside from Seth's intermittent stabs at making conversation. Charlotte knew she wasn't making it easy on him, and it wasn't as if any of this were his fault. But she couldn't manage talking. Not yet.

"Do you want to ride out to FAO Schwarz?" he asked. "You mentioned wanting to check it out. Maybe we could have dinner in the city."

"No. I just want to—"

She didn't know what she wanted to do.

Scream. Throw a tantrum. Set Angelica Windom's hair on fire and watch her burn.

"—have a quiet night."

"All right," he said, and they drove on in silence.

Back at the brownstone, it was more of the same, and when Seth could take it no more, he came up behind where she stood at the window and placed his arms around her waist.

"What is it, darling?"

"I'm just so tired." She wasn't lying. "I'm tired down to my bones."

"Why don't you stretch out across the bed for a while then?" he said. "I'll put something together for dinner."

"Maybe I will," she replied, but didn't move.

"Seth?" she whispered after a long break of silence.

"Hmmmm?"

"Remember last night when you were telling me about Fulton House and how much it means to you?"

"Yes."

"What would it do to you if the deal fell apart? I mean, what would you do?"

"Don't even think that way, Ms. Dennison," he whispered into her ear. "It's all set."

"But what if—"

"Don't say it," he said. "Don't even utter the words. I couldn't stand to lose it all now. It means more to me than almost anything."

More than me?

She waited in vain for him to speak the words.

"Why this doom and gloom?" he asked instead. "I won't hear any of it, do you understand? Nothing's going to happen to that project that doesn't involve making money and reaping infinite amounts of reward. You go rest, and I'll call you for dinner."

Charlotte tried to relax her body, without success. It all crashed over her in thunderous waves as she rolled to her other side—Angelica's threats, Seth's enthusiasm for the project. And although it burned her from the inside out to think about it, she could do nothing else. The voices and scenarios streaked across her consciousness like acid rain.

If she told him, Seth would confront the witch. Of that, Charlotte was certain. Seth was that kind of man. And then, before the dust settled, Angelica would undoubtedly pull the plug on Fulton House.

If she left him, Seth would have the project he adored, and all the certain success that would come with it. But they would be apart, both of them miserable. And could she even convince him that everything between them had been a lie, that she didn't love him, that there was anything about him or their future that was significant enough to cause her to leave?

Perhaps she could go to Windom himself. Present her case, tell him what his daughter was trying to do, beg him not to let her take away everything Seth had worked so hard to attain. . . . No. That wasn't an option.

Lorette.

If only she could just talk the situation through with Lorette. She'd know what to do.

But Charlotte already knew what her friend would tell her. Forget the project, viva l'amour! Everything else in the world took a second seat to love as far as Lorette was concerned, and Charlotte knew she couldn't possibly understand how important Fulton House was to Seth, how long he'd worked, the level of faith he'd forced himself to maintain. He couldn't lose it all now. And if he did, he would never be able to look at Charlotte again without remembering that she was the one who had caused the bottom to fall out on his dream.

Seth would never tell her to go. Not in a million years would he take the low road and think only of himself. In fact, everything Seth did in life was done with consideration for the feelings of others. Fulton House was the one and only thing that was his alone, and she couldn't allow him to lose it. Not because of her.

But how in the world would she ever walk away from him? Her love was so strong that she wasn't sure she would ever be able to do anything so noble.

Do I love Seth enough to give him up? she asked herself, and she wasn't the least bit surprised at the answer.

I don't know if I can.

* * *

Dinner would have been nothing less than scrumptious under any other circumstances, but it was all Charlotte could do to keep herself planted at the table and pick at the shrimp salad.

"It looks like you may get that snow you were hoping for," Seth told her, and she forced a smile.

"Charlotte, aren't you feeling well?"

"No," she told him truthfully. "I'm really not."

"Do you need a doctor?"

"No. I'll be fine."

"Have I done something to upset you?" he asked, and her heart wrenched at the way his eyes misted over with emotion.

She was breaking his heart, she knew that. And she couldn't put a stop to it.

"Charlotte?" Then he repeated, "Are you upset with me?"

"No."

Seth stared at her so hard that it stirred the acid in her stomach.

"Will you talk to me? What is wrong?"

"Nothing."

He paused for a moment, then tossed his fork down into his salad bowl and jumped to his feet. It was the loudest clearing of a table she had ever heard.

"I'll be in my study," he snapped at her, then disappeared from the room and slammed shut the door down the hall.

Charlotte couldn't blame him for being angry. She was the one who had forced their relationship by showing up in New York, and now the one thing she couldn't do was just talk to him, tell him the truth.

She knew Seth, the kind of man he was who would fight for what was right, stand up for justice no matter what the cost. And in his taking a stand, he would effectively hang himself with his own rope—if she let him. And she would not let him.

She busied herself with the dishes, and she wiped the counters at least three times before realizing they didn't need any more attention.

When night fell and Seth had not emerged from his study, Charlotte climbed into the guest room bed without saying a word to him. She felt so alone, and it was a cold, harsh alone, more biting than any she had ever known. The huge bed felt like miles of sheets and blankets, not a warm body or an easy smile anywhere on the horizon, and Charlotte turned her face into the pillow and began to cry in grievous, uncontrollable sobs.

She was going to lose Seth.

The reality dropped on her like tons of concrete and brick. Any way it went, she was going to lose him. And there wasn't a thing she could do to prevent it.

Charlotte awoke to the rhythmic sound of Seth's breathing, and she saw him curled into the chair beside her bed. She rolled over toward him, her cheek buried in the damp, tear-stained pillow, and watched him for a long while.

"Oh, God," she whispered. "What am I going to do?"

Under any other circumstances, she might ask Seth for advice. But neither Seth nor Lorette nor any other person on the face of the earth could dig up the answers for her. She would have to forge out the solution on her own, and she wished she didn't keep coming back to murdering Angelica as a viable option.

As the voices turned over in her mind for the millionth time, something dropped in the pit of Charlotte's stomach. There was no other solution but the obvious. Angelica had won, as she knew she would. The witch had won.

No matter how many angles Charlotte experimented with, she could not get past the one truth at the center of it all.

The Fulton House project.

It was Seth's whole life, his future, and she couldn't let him lose it. Maybe in a year or two, after he was out of harm's way and Angelica's reign of terror was past, perhaps they could find each other again. Perhaps . . .

But she couldn't allow herself to think that way, and she banished the hope from her mind. Just six short months ago, she had her whole future in line. She was going to see the world. Venice was waiting, she reminded herself. She was going to move up the corporate ladder at Global, and she'd already put in applications for jobs in the company outside of Reservations. Something was bound to come along for her. Something with more money, to help with the care her father required.

She hadn't wanted or needed a man in her life just six months ago. She never dreamed of the path she had taken with Seth since then. If she could just get back to that time. If she could just find her way back to when being alone didn't matter.

Charlotte looked at Seth's face and started to cry once more. She had stepped down the path with him. The yellow brick road had led her happily here to Oz, and the truth was there was no place like home, like the one she could only find in the safety of his arms.

It broke Charlotte's heart to get out of that bed. She thought it would kill her as she gathered her things and silently packed them into the overnight case. She left the scribbled note on the kitchen counter and fought like a banshee against the sobs that wanted to take over her entire body as she slid into her coat and stepped outside into the cold night air, looking upward into a pitch-black sky.

"Take care of him, God," she whispered as she picked up her bag and walked down to the street. "Keep him safe and warm and happy."

Tears felt as if they would freeze to her face as she tread slowly down the sidewalk, and just as the taxi pulled to a slippery stop at the curb, the first snowflakes began to fall from the heavens.

"Kennedy Airport, please," she mumbled as she slid into the back seat.

"We're gonna have a good couple of inches before morning," the driver announced. "Looks like you're leavin' town just in the knick of time."

You have no idea.

She was silent in the back of the cab. It was, after all, very difficult to make polite conversation while her heart was shattering inside her.

Chapter Seventeen

The phone messages kept coming, half a dozen of them every day. Seth, wondering what had happened, what had he done wrong, couldn't they work it out? Then the letters, two in the first week, and another a while after that.

He called Lorette, asking her to explain it to him, to intervene. But Lorette had already fought the issue for days on end, pleading with Charlotte to tell him the truth, to let him help make the horror of it right again. But Charlotte had refused, and Lorette finally agreed to keep the secret. And so Lorette turned Seth away with the advice that he let it drop. It was over. A terrible mistake finally realized. Charlotte was heartbroken that she'd hurt him, but it was really all for the best.

And then she and Charlotte cried together all that night. They cried for the lie, and they cried for Seth, and most of all they cried for Charlotte, a requiem for the one true love of her life, hopelessly lost.

Charlotte's world fell silent the moment that Seth did. The Christmas gift he'd sent still sat on the floor of her living room, unopened. Christmas had come and gone, as had their six-month wedding anniversary.

The checks still came from Seth, an even $1,000 at the first of each month, and she filed them away in the bottom drawer of her bureau, atop a pile of other envelopes in his handwriting, bound together with a crisp blue ribbon. She wanted him to continue making use of her travel benefits for as long as he needed them, but she couldn't take his money—not even for her father's care. She simply couldn't bring herself to cash the checks. The struggle to make the payments without them had been dramatic, but she'd managed.

Without Seth's support, though, it was painfully clear that her father wouldn't be able to stay at Heathcliffe; notwithstanding, there was also her own situation to consider. She'd rented the house depending on Seth money each month, and that no longer was so. The night she made the decision to move out was the night she finally packed the remnants of Seth.

The first to see the inside of the cardboard box was the framed and matted gift from Lorette. Seth never got a chance to see it. Charlotte scanned the verse written in large block letters.

"For love is strong as death," she read aloud, then wiped the tears from her eyes.

It only feels like death.

Next came the black leather jacket she'd never gotten around to returning, and the framed photos of the two of them on the dresser and the mantel. The last to go was the most difficult—Mr. Scuff-Shoes.

Once the box was closed up, Charlotte picked it up and headed straight to the trash at the side of the house. She took a ragged, solid breath, then dropped the thing into the can and headed back toward the house.

But Charlotte froze as she reached for the front door. She couldn't do it, she just couldn't. But why not? Seth had stopped calling and writing. It was as if he had disappeared from the face of the earth except for the checks. So why couldn't she?

She didn't know. She just couldn't.

She ran to the back of the house and retrieved the box from the trash. Then, with a slower gait, she made her way to the garage and let herself inside, the box clutched to her chest as she placed it on the shelf next to the gardening utensils and her old record collection.

She walked slowly back to the house, gazing up at the stars in the navy sky. She considered that Seth might be looking up at the very same stars, and she scolded herself before hurrying inside.

She needed to keep busy, she decided. She flipped on the radio to keep her company while she scrubbed the bathroom.

"Goin' to the chapel and we're gonna get ma-a-arried, goin' to the chapel and we're . . ."

She flicked it off. Maybe the television instead.

Two hours later, Charlotte had a cleaner bathroom, kitchen, and pantry than any woman in Georgia. If only she were tired enough to go to sleep, she groaned to herself.

She hadn't brewed a cup of vanilla almond tea in the three months since she and Seth had parted, and despite her intense craving for it now, she snatched a large bottle of Mountain Dew from the fridge and a package of Oreos from the freezer, collapsing in front of the television.

One cookie led to several, and before she knew it, the package was empty and Charlotte dropped the empty plastic jug over the side of the sofa.

Yuck. What have I done to myself?

* * *

The morning sun burned cruelly and unusually hot on Charlotte's face as it blazed its way through the front window. She glanced at the overturned Mountain Dew container on the coffee table as a familiar jingle droned on annoyingly in the background.

What day is it?

Reality smacked Charlotte hard in the jaw, and she jumped up from the sofa so quickly that she fell right back down again.

"Tuesday!" she screamed, then forced herself to her feet and ran to her bedroom.

"Ten o'clock!" she shrieked, slamming her fist down on top of the sirening alarm clock. How long had it been wailing?

For over an hour!

Her appointment with Mike Jansen was at eleven, and she'd never make it if her nausea won.

Charlotte stood under the cool shower for an extra long time, struggling to gain control of her reeling senses. She could almost hear Lorette's logic bouncing around the walls inside her head. Telling her how she'd been punishing herself, that she actually feared the success this meeting might have and so she had deliberately, albeit unconsciously, sabotaged herself.

"Oh, shut up!" she yelled out loud, then quickly plugged in the blow dryer.

When she finally appeared in Jansen's office, the clock on his wall read 11:03.

"Charlotte Dennison-Pruitt to see Mike Jansen," she announced to the secretary, and then followed the woman's wave toward one of the reception chairs.

She desperately wanted this job. The additional income would allow her to stay in the house she had come to love so much, and a move from Reservations would be timely for her indeed. She needed something else to think about, something new to focus on.

"Frankly, Ms. Pruitt," Jansen told her once the formalities were dispensed, "one of the things that made us take a second look at your application was your stability. You're married, you have roots. It looks like you're going to stick with us for a while."

Charlotte pasted a smile over her worry lines. "I've learned all I feel I can learn in Reservations," she told him. "I'm ready to move on to something that challenges me."

"New horizons to conquer and all that," he said. "I like that kind of cautious ambition in a Global employee. My only concern, Charlotte, is that I've caught wind of a rumor."

Her heart stopped beating, and she waited what felt like three days for him to finish.

"About your husband."

"My husband?" she asked innocently.

"The two of you were married rather quickly," he went on. "And some people have been talking. You know, just the water cooler banter, really. But they're saying there is more to your marriage than meets the eye."

"Oh?"

How could anyone know?

"They're saying you married him as a business deal, so that he could take advantage of Global's spousal travel privileges."

She suddenly felt faint.

"I've said this is utter nonsense. No one with the potential that Charlotte Dennison-Pruitt has here at Global would take such a risk with their job. Such a fraudulent move would be doing just that, Ms. Pruitt. Had you done such a careless thing, you could be fired."

"Yes," she said as she reached for her confidence mask. "Of course I could, Mr. Jansen. But that's not the situation."

"It isn't." It seemed more like a statement than a question.

"No, of course not. My husband and I admittedly married very fast. If I'm guilty of a careless act, that would be it. We should have taken more time, gotten to know each other. We're paying the price for it now, though, as we work through the getting-to-know-you phase of our relationship. It's not as easy as we might have thought."

"It never is," he said, laughing good-naturedly.

"We'll work it out," she tried to smile. "There is some distance between us because of his job."

"Yes, of course," he said, nodding almost sympathetically. "I remember hearing that."

"In any case, you needn't worry about my job performance being affected. I've been married for months now, and if you'll check my record you'll see that I have performed flawlessly in spite of it."

At the close of their hour-long meeting, Jansen informed Charlotte that it could be two weeks before a decision was made, but she was definately a forerunner for the new position in the Quality Control division. It would involve extensive travel, but her salary would increase by almost 50 percent.

"So I'd travel from one vacation spot to another," she explained to Lorette as she prepared a pot of cinnamon coffee. "Like an anonymous shopper, checking out the treatment a regular passenger gets in first class, how the tour package is put together, the quality of the hotels included in the tour."

"All you'll do is travel, then? Don't you get to stay in one place?"

"Yes," she explained. "That's the beauty of it. I'll be here in the Atlanta office two or three weeks out of the month, and I'll be traveling the rest of the time. If I get the job, my first assignment is on a package tour to Mexico!"

"I'm going to miss you," Lorette told her seriously.

"I haven't got the job yet, silly," she said, then hugged her friend. "You've already got me halfway around the world."

"So when will you know?"

"Mr. Jansen said it could be a couple of weeks."

Which is why Charlotte was so very surprised when she received the call the next morning offering her the job, effective immediately.

The first week in Quality Control was much harder than Charlotte anticipated, and she realized she never appreciated her job in Reservations for routine. Plug in, answer the phone, be polite, and take reservations. Once she'd learned the codes and was familiar with the computer system, it had become rather mindless in many ways.

The new job would never take on that quality. The requirements were much higher in terms of the duties as well as the time she would have to put in.

Mike Jansen was a good guy to work for, and he took a lot of extra time with Charlotte in the first week—introducing her, supplying her with hints and reference materials and suggestions on how to deal with the different personalities in his department.

She would take part in the seven-day tour as an average traveler, and no one besides Mike would know her true mission. She would take notes and fill out reports at the end of each day offering her recommendations. She would call in every morning to discuss her findings and Mike would give her an instant critique of her work and suggest ways she might see things differently or approach a given situation more effectively. Mike promised her she would be an old hand at Quality Control by the time he was through with her, and she believed him.

Even more importantly, though, she was looking forward to the new challenge, and planned to gain as much knowledge from her new mentor as possible. Mike had taken her under his wing, and she knew right away that he was the person to know if she wanted to learn everything about her new job.

This was more than just a good opportunity. The job was the first stone in the path she'd always planned for her future, for her father's future.

Her thoughts were filled with packing and arrangements and forms to fill out as she pulled into the driveway that night. The last thing on earth she expected to find at her door was Seth Pruitt!

Chapter Eighteen

"How are you, Charlotte?"

Seth had changed quite a bit. His hair was shorter, and the lines on his face seemed deeper, more intense. But his eyes were still the bluest she'd ever seen, and it was the most restraint she had ever exercised not to race into his arms.

"Seth. What are you doing here?"

"Can I come in?" he asked solemnly. "I'd like to talk to you."

"Of course."

Charlotte noticed that Seth was looking around him attentively as they entered the living room. There was no trace of their prior life together anywhere in the house, she had made certain of that, and she wondered if he noticed.

"Would you like coffee or something? Tea?"

"No," he replied politely. "Thank you, but I won't be staying long."

Charlotte lowered herself into the wingback chair and waited.

"You haven't been cashing my checks," he stated.

"No, I haven't. Under the circumstances, I didn't think—"

"Yes, well," he interrupted her. "Regardless of the circumstances, the agreement was that you would get the cash and I would get the travel. I'm thinking that it might be time to . . . terminate our arrangement."

Charlotte wasn't entirely certain what he meant, and she guessed he realized that from the look on her face.

"A divorce," he explained. "I think it's time we divorce."

The notion cut her heart open like a sharp blade.

"Oh."

It was all she could manage for the moment.

A divorce.

The word hung in the air, a toxin that sucked the very life from the room.

"I have a new job at Global," she said, and hoped he hadn't noticed the way she struggled to form the words. "Quality Control. And I'm going on my first project assignment next week."

"That's wonderful for you, Charlotte. It's just what you wanted. This is a perfect time to end it then."

"How has the Fulton House project worked out for you?" She had to ask. "Has construction begun yet?"

"Yes. We should see a grand opening sometime in the next two months. We've already begun the negotiations for some land in Dallas and Seattle for the next two."

"Windom and Pruitt," she swallowed bitterly. "Quite the team."

"Yes. Well, we're finished then," he cut her off. "I'll call you in a day or two to finalize the arrangements."

At that moment, the phone rang, and it seemed louder than usual, like a siren steam-rolling right through her.

"I'll let you . . ." he began, then started for the door.

"No!' she blurted, then took a deep breath she hoped would be cleansing. Instead, it was ragged and cut bitterly into her chest. "Wait a moment, please."

He politely acquiesced, but she could see he was anxious to leave.

"Yes," she answered. "Hello?"

"Charlotte, it's Mike. We have a problem."

She had to force herself to concentrate on his words as she watched Seth shift from one foot to the other, absently running his finger over the framed photo of her father on the end table beside her favorite wingback chair.

An investigation . . . job status pending . . . marriage in question . . .

"What?" she finally cried. "Mike, wait a minute! What are you saying?"

The alarm in her voice served as a summons to Seth, and he appeared immediately at her side.

"It's come as a directive from one of the Global board members," he said with a sigh. "They plan to use you as the sacrificial lamb, Charlotte. I'm sorry. Selling benefits is a serious offense against the company. If you and Seth married for any other reason than mad and passionate love—"

"We didn't," she lied. "It's not true!"

"I know, Charlotte. But there's going to be an investigation. Once it's proven that you two are a legitimate happy couple, the world will spin again and your job status will be reinstated. Until then, I'm afraid . . ." He trailed off sadly.

"What does this mean?" she asked, her eyes quickly diverting from Seth's serious gaze. "Am I out of a job? Am I back in Reservations? What?"

"You're still a member of the Quality Control team," he told her. "But the Mexico trip is off. I'll assign Desmond."

"Yes," she said as she rubbed a hand tiredly through her hair. "He'll be great."

"I know you're disappointed," he tried to encourage her. "You'll be out there in no time at all doing the job you were hired to do. In the meantime, you'll work on scheduling and assignments."

"Right," she said half-heartedly. "Thanks for calling me, Mike."

"I didn't want you to find out here at the office," he said. "I thought it would be better this way."

"It is. Thanks."

"See you in the morning?"

"Yes."

Charlotte hung up the phone carefully before pounding her fist hard against the counter. Tears rose into her eyes, and her heart was beating so hard that her chest ached.

"What is it?"

She'd forgotten Seth was there.

"Your promotion?" he asked.

"What promotion?" she returned sarcastically.

"No." He seemed to drop in spirit as hard as she had.

"They're initiating an investigation."

"Into what?"

"Into our marriage," she told him bitterly. "To see if I married you only to sell my company benefits."

"Oh, Charlotte. No."

"Yes. And if I have, my career at Global comes in for a serious crash landing."

"What can we do?"

"We?"

He'd said it so matter-of-factly that it surprised her. "You were asking me for a divorce ten minutes ago, Seth."

She wanted to laugh at the irony, but she didn't have a chuckle left inside her.

"I'd say the circumstances warrant a bit of spontaneity here, wouldn't you?"

His smile was warm, and she felt its heat in the arches of her feet.

"We'll do what we have to for the moment," he told her. "And take care of the other details later."

He barely gave an instant's notice before wrapping her up in his arms. The embrace though unexpected was welcome and comforting, and Charlotte made no move to pull away from it. She nuzzled further into him, in fact, as he smoothed her hair down her back with the palm of his hand.

"We'll take care of everything," he whispered. She didn't know why she believed him just then, but she did. "Everything will be okay."

Charlotte prayed the news of their trip would not reach Angelica Windom as the wheels touched the runway of Charles De Gaulle Airport.

It had seemed like a good idea when she and Seth discussed the advantages of attending the departmental retreat in Paris. All the bigwigs would be in attendance, many of them with their spouses, and seeing Charlotte and Seth as a happy married couple could only prove beneficial.

Many of the people making the final decision on Charlotte's future were with them, Mike had pointed out at some point on the seven-hour flight from Kennedy to Paris.

"Susan Conklin," he'd said with the covert arch of his brow that one could expect from a secret agent briefing his team. "She's the gal who started it all. She'll be the toughest nut to crack."

The woman had the intimidating appearance of a high school principal—reddish hair which curled obediently into a twist at the back of her head, and prim little horn-rimmed glasses which sat curtly at the edge of her bony nose.

Charlotte couldn't help noticing earlier in the flight when she rose from her seat and followed Seth to the magazine rack at the front of the cabin.

She strained to hear the details of the apparently polite banter between the two of them, and she couldn't help but grin at the adept timing of those magnetic smiles Seth bestowed on her at just the right moments. The woman's flashes of girlish response warmed Charlotte to her soul. Those smiles of Seth's were a gift, there was no denying that, and she was happy and grateful that he'd chosen to make effective use of them on her behalf.

Using them for good rather than evil, she told herself, then suppressed the laughter that bubbled to the surface.

Those smiles were a sword with which he'd begun to battle her dragons.

When Charlotte had first mentioned the Paris trip to Seth, it had been to ask his creative assistance in concocting a suitable explanation for his absence, not convince him to pose as the ecstatic groom on the other half of her wedding cake. But he had jumped on the idea of using the trip to their advantage, and he'd been very persuasive in bringing her to his way of thinking.

"If you want out of this marriage as badly as you seemed to the day you walked out of my brownstone and out of my life," he'd said, "then this is a step in that direction."

"Seth, I . . ." she'd begun, but he'd cut her off with the wave of his hand.

"No explanations are necessary, Ms. Dennison," and he managed to smile. "Your note was short and sweet, but the point was in no way lost on me. So, we secure your job and then you can easily afford the divorce when it eventually comes about."

Charlotte had looked at him after he said that for a long moment. She wanted to explain so many things: about Angelica, about how much their time together in New York meant to her, what *he* meant to her.

She wanted desperately to tell him about the lonely nights which had eaten her alive since she'd walked out of that brownstone. But she didn't. Fulton House and his dreams surrounding it were like a carefully constructed house of cards to her just then, and one word from her could bring the breeze that could cave them in for good. So she remained silent. And the silence was so loud that it hurt her ears.

"No job, no income," Seth had said. "And no income—where does that leave your dad?"

He knew how to drive a point home, that was for sure. Charlotte hadn't taken long after that to agree to a short sham of a "second honeymoon" to continue life without him.

Without his money, she reminded herself. But it was living without Seth that posed the deepest challenge for Charlotte.

She shook the thoughts forcibly from her mind as the "fasten seat belt" sign went off and the cabin around them turned to a bustle of activity. Seth's hand on her back was her lifeline, and she let him lead her down the ramp and into the airport.

Checking into the hotel was a breeze, and the bellman was quick and polite in guiding them through the winding halls to their room at Hotel de L'Université.

As Charlotte situated herself behind the desk to sort through the list of tours their group might take while in Paris, Seth busied himself with hanging up a suit jacket from the garment bag and unloading toiletries noisily to the counter in the bathroom.

"So what's on the itinerary for tomorrow?" he asked as he suddenly appeared before her and perched at the edge of the writing desk.

"A few hours at the Louvre," she read to him. "Then the Eiffel Tower in the afternoon."

His grimace disapproved.

"No?" she asked curiously.

"No! The doors open at nine forty-five in the morning and close at six-thirty p.m. If you spend every moment in between running from wall to wall, you still would never see everything worth seeing."

"You've been here before," she stated.

"Once or twice," he replied "Let's make our own tour. We'll spend the day, see everything we can. And we can have lunch at Cafe Marly. The outdoor terrace looks out at Pei's glass pyramid in the main esplanade."

"But, Seth, we're here to put on a show. If we go off on our own, what good will that do?"

"So we'll invite some of the key players to join us. There's nothing like the Eiffel Tower at night, Charlotte."

"You can go there at night? I don't remember that!"

"Yes. It's magnificent."

"We'll organize an intimate group to take the elevator up to the top tonight, then we'll hold hands, we'll bat our eyes at each other, and tomorrow you'll have ample time to completely enjoy what the Louvre has to offer."

"Sounds like a good plan," she said. "You'll invite your friend, Susan Conklin, of course."

Seth stretched tightened his lips into a proper purse. "But of course I will." And his imitation of the old biddy was close to perfect.

Charlotte couldn't remember when the tension in her

stomach finally dissipated, but she noticed it when she and Seth both burst into laughter. It felt so good to laugh with him again. It had been far too long.

The last time he'd seen Paris from the inside of a taxi, Seth had been dreadfully unhappy. The ride that rainy afternoon had been one of the longest of his life. Now, looking over at Charlotte, all smiles in anticipation for the sights and sounds, the city looked fresher somehow than the first time around.

Her eyes met his for an instant, and her smile was a fire that ignited him.

"Seth, it's so beautiful, isn't it?" she said, and he reached over and took her hand into his, raising it to his lips for a quick kiss that he told himself was for the sake of the others who were watching them so closely.

"Seth, you seem to know the city quite well," Rita, Mike's wife, said as she leaned back over the front seat of the cab. "Have you spent much time here?"

"I spent six months here out of college," he told them as he met Charlotte's gaze. "In a former life."

"That's very mysterious," Susan remarked.

"Every guy has a mystery or two in his past," said Mike from the other side of Seth, with a chuckle.

"Oh really?" his wife inquired from the front seat.

"Uh-oh," Mike said, then they all laughed.

"Seth was here with an old flame," Charlotte told them when they had fallen quiet and still waited for his unwilling response. She looked at him for a moment. "A very tragic story," she added. "She broke his heart."

Seth's stomach lurched, and his brow was covered instantly in a mist of perspiration.

How could she have known?

He quickly scanned their past conversations, like a computer program searching for a keyword to identify a passage of text, but he came up empty.

A flicker of light twinkled at him as she smiled, and he tried to return it but knew that the effort had produced more of a grimace than a grin.

"There it is!" Rita gasped, and Seth was relieved when all attention moved from him to the sight before them.

"Oh . . . Seth! It's more beautiful than I remembered."

Charlotte's enchantment with the majesty of the Eiffel Towel brought a shiver to him. She had a way of making him see the world differently.

"Shall we tour first and stop in at the restaurant after?" someone suggested, and it was unamimously agreed upon.

Charlotte seemed to Seth like a dazzled child on Christmas morning as she slipped her little hand into his and shuffled wide-eyed behind the others.

"Isn't that right, Seth?"

He hadn't heard her question, and Seth grinned at Susan, stalling.

"Around what? 1860?" she hinted.

Like a glimmer of light in his self-inflicted darkness, he snatched onto the clue and ran with it.

"1889," he corrected, confident to be back with the program. "La Tour Eiffel," he told them in his best French accent. "Contruite par l'ingenieur Gustave Eiffel pour l'Exposition Universelle."

"Oooooh," Susan squealed. "You enunciate perfectly!"

"And for those of us who struggle with the English language?" Rita teased. "Translation?"

"Oh." Susan grinned and touched Seth's arm as if the two of them shared a private joke. "He was saying that the tower was built in 1889," she explained, like a kindergarten teacher talking to her students. "Constructed by Gustave

Eiffel, a very famous French engineer, for the World Exhibition being held in Paris that year. Isn't that right, Seth?"

"Oui," he replied sweetly before moving ahead of them, Charlotte's hand still firmly in his.

"There's a tea room here I know you'd love," he told Charlotte, and her smile told him that his reference to knowing her tastes was not lost on her. He was well aware that all eyes and ears were back on them. "It's called Le Parisien. Unfortunately, it's not open tonight. La Belle France is open, though. We can have a couple of drinks there later."

"Aperitif," Susan added, and Seth nodded politely.

If this woman was the toughest thing standing between Charlotte and her job, he knew they had already triumphed. The problem was with triumph also came completion. Mission accomplished. And then where would they be?

The view from the top of the tower never grew old to Seth. Paris spread out beneath them like a night sky filled with stars. The City of Lights it was indeed. An endless, amazing canvas in different degrees of luminescence. It reminded him of Charlotte. Bright and brilliant in some areas, muted and pastel in others, but 100 percent shimmering light just the same.

"It's incredible," she whispered, and he smiled.

Stepping up beside him, she welcomed his arm as it moved instinctively around her.

"How did you know?"

The question was out before he was even aware that it had sprung to mind, and Charlotte cocked her head in that familiar and quite adorable way she had when sizing up something he'd said.

"When you told them I'd been to Paris before."

"Oh, that," she said, then let out a tiny giggle.

"Oh that," he teased.

"I don't know. I just did."

Her reply didn't surprise him. Sometimes Seth felt as if he had no secrets when he was with this woman. Like he went walking through life wearing an overcoat only she had the power to see beyond. There was nothing hidden between them, and he vacillated between awe of that quality in her and a sort of fear of it.

It went beyond just the mind-reading thing, too. He couldn't quite explain the connection. It was as if he were holding a cord, the plug draped casually across his hand as he went through life just waiting for the moment when he might stumble upon that one socket that was just the right fit.

In Charlotte he'd found that. It scared him how much in step the two of them were, how in tune. No one had ever been able to complete the connection for him like that before. Not even Michele.

"Was she very beautiful?"

She was reading his mind again.

"Yes. She was."

She pondered his reply.

"She had the darkest eyes I'd ever seen," he began, but wasn't quite sure why. "And long, shiny black hair."

"And she broke your heart," she stated. "Is she why you never married? Before me."

"I suppose," he said. "I never really thought about it."

Charlotte faced him squarely. "Did you bring her here to Paris?"

"She lived here," he said, although talking about it again after such a very long time was excruciating. And yet he was strangely compelled to continue.

"We were very much in love. Planning to be married here in Paris, and then she was going to move back to the States with me."

"What happened?" Charlotte took his hand and looked deeply into his eyes.

"One day we were sitting in a little cafe on the Champs Elysées." He paused to take in a deep, ragged breath. "And she tells me she's had a change of heart. She doesn't want to leave Paris. I was thrown at first . . ."

"I told her we could make some adjustments," he continued. "I could look for work here. And then she told me . . . she'd had a change of heart about me, too."

"Oh, Seth. Did you ever see her again?"

"No."

He wiped the dampness from his eyes before turning to face her. "I wrote to her for years, but she never answered. Then a couple of years ago, I came back on business, and went to her house."

"Was she happy to see you? After all the years, surely . . ."

"She didn't live there any more," he explained. "I did some checking and finally found Noelle, her best friend."

"And did she lead you to her?"

"Yes," he said, the emotion overtaking him again.

He hesitated. "She had died that summer."

"Oh, Seth!" Charlotte gasped, then pulled him roughly into an embrace.

"It seems they had discovered cancer in her body," he continued, then broke free of Charlotte and turned to face the calling splendor of Paris beneath them. "She didn't want me to face that with her, so she'd sent me back home to the States without her. To believe that she'd rejected me, so that she could face her demons . . . alone."

Seth held himself stiffly, his back upright as he faced away from Charlotte. He hoped his frame would not betray him, and he wiped away the tears that glided down his face, then worked hard to suppress the sobs which battled so desperately to accompany them.

"And yet," she whispered, one hand flat to his back, gently massaging, "you came back here for me."

"I couldn't be there for Michele," he said as he turned back toward her. "You needed me to do this. And your father needed it, too."

"Seth . . ."

The two came together into a kiss that washed over Seth like a hot waterfall. He'd been wanting to kiss her like that for months, dreaming of it at night, imagining it most days. And ever since he'd discovered months of her uncashed checks while going over his books, he'd been drowning in the notion that the end of their so-called marriage and the end of his hopes for a moment like this one was near. Her in his arms. Their lips pressed hard together.

"Well, well, well." Susan cackled. "I think we can put those rumors to rest. Don't you think so, Mike?"

"Doesn't look like the kiss of an arranged marriage to me," her boss replied with a wink, and Seth felt Charlotte's radiance.

"Are we ready for that nightcap?" Rita asked, and they all nodded.

"Let's go," Seth said, then put an arm around Charlotte.

It wasn't his imagination when she squirmed suddenly from his touch and hurried ahead to Rita's side. Seth watched her for a moment, wondering what had just happened there. Perhaps she was simply embarrassed, but it seemed like much more than that to him. He felt like he had been kicked in his stomach.

As they entered the elevator, her gaze met everything except his.When the doors slid open, she hurried from the car so quickly she nearly left marks on the floor.

So much for that hope he'd felt rekindled inside him.

This girl was dripping with the fluid of regret since the moment their kiss had ended. He might not be the Einstein of women and relationships, but Seth Pruitt knew one thing for sure. He knew when he was being brushed off.

It was the moment Charlotte had been dreading all evening, and there had been no stopping it. The return to their room, the heat of that kiss still ablaze within her.

They'd said their good-nights several times over, and she'd even tried to extend the evening by inviting Mike and Rita back for coffee. But there was nothing stopping it now.

"Would you like to use the bathroom first?" he asked.

She silently cursed Seth for his oblivious return to life.

He had nothing more to think about than that while she flailed hopelessly, drowning in her desire for him, an inferno from a kiss she'd been dreaming about for months!

"No. You go ahead."

Wordlessly, he stepped out of sight and closed the door, although she could feel his continuing presence as keenly as if he were standing right beside her.

Every time she lost herself in thoughts of reconciliation, in momentary dreams of a future with this man she had come to love so much, Angelica's face would pop up as if on a video screen in front of her. And behind Angelica were all of Seth's dreams, noisily crumbling to dust.

Charlotte pounded her fist on the writing table. What if she just told him? What if she just confessed the whole truth? That she loved him. That she didn't want to lose him again. That she . . .

"Just tell me one thing! What was that? Pity?"

"What?" she cried. His reappearance in the room startled her to instant tears.

"You felt sorry for me, is that it? Because I'll tell you

something, Charlotte, that didn't seem like the kiss of someone who felt nothing more for me than pity."

"No . . . I . . . uh . . ."

No words. Not a single one. Her mind was a complete blank.

"Are you going to answer? What are you thinking, Charlotte?"

She turned away from him and focused on the tail light of a plane making its way through the midnight sky.

"Because you're killing me," he said in a raspy voice.

She turned to face him, startled at the emotion in his eyes.

"I'm so in love with you, I can hardly see straight, Ms. Dennison. Don't you know that?"

"I . . . no. I didn't."

"I thought you . . . that you'd begun to . . . What happened with us, Charlotte?"

He looked like a frightened child before her, his hair tousled and his eyes misted over, stripped bare of all his adult masks and veils.

"I love you," he said, and it broke her heart right in two.

"Oh, Seth, don't. Let's not do this."

"No, let's do, Charlotte," he shouted, pulling her to him. "Let's do this now. Right here, right now, you look me straight in the eye and tell me you don't love me, too."

She tried to look at him, but the intensity of his stare drove her gaze away immediately.

"Let go."

"Charlotte," he said, loosening his grasp but still holding her to him.

She looked back again, this time locking into his sights and unable to break free.

"Tell me you don't love me," he pleaded. "Tell me. It will release me, I swear to God. Let me hear it, Charlotte."

"I . . . can't," she finally said, darting her eyes away.

"Then why? Why have you been avoiding me like a virus? And why did you leave me that morning at the brownstone?"

"You'd better ask Angelica."

The words finally out, she felt nothing except a very low-grade relief.

"Angelica?" he repeated. "Angelica Windom? What's she got to do with this? I haven't even seen her in months."

"What?"

"What does Angelica have to do with us?" he demanded.

"She told me if I didn't walk away, Fulton House would fold."

"She—what?"

Seth's eyes flickered with a zillion different scenarios. "She what?" he repeated. "When?"

"At the gym," she told him. "Remember that she was there?"

"My God, Charlotte, Angelica has been out of the Fulton House project for at least six weeks now."

Charlotte gasped. "What?"

"She just began taking too much control. Making decisions that weren't hers to make. It became unbearable, and finally . . . I walked."

"You didn't. Seth, all your hard work."

"Hard work is rewarded, isn't that what you used to tell me? When they found out what happened, MacGregor and Barnes brought a group of investors together and came to me. We've formed a limited partnership and are going ahead with an international franchise on Fulton House Inns."

"Oh, Seth!" she cried, clasping his hand. "Can we really pick up and go on now?"

"Can we do anything else?" he asked her.

"If only I'd known," she said tearfully.

"I've spent the last several months saying, 'If only,' Charlotte. If only I'd known what made you so unhappy, if only I'd done something differently, if only I could get you back."

"Seth."

"Come back to me now," he said softly.

"Yes."

And the two of them came together in a heated kiss.

Chapter Nineteen

Seth's car pulled into the driveway, and Charlotte frantically made sure everything was in place, then hid in the pantry. Since he had moved his business to Atlanta, he hadn't come home late a single day. Today was no different, and for that she said a silent thank-you.

"Ms. Dennison?" he called as he came in the door, mail in hand.

Charlotte struggled to remain quiet. It was all she could do not to explode with the good news.

"Honey?"

She clasped a hand over her mouth and closed her eyes. He was in the kitchen, she could tell, but why didn't he say anything? Hadn't he seen it?

Charlotte carefully poked her head around the corner to find him standing over the note where she'd left it, folded in half so that it sat upright on the kitchen table:

Wanted: Caring man with scuffed shoes and sky-blue eyes for ultimate challenge. Must be madly in love with his wife and have a true heart for children. Interested in supporting your wife for the next six months while she carries your baby? Then this is the marriage to be in.

Seth reeled around so quickly that he almost lost his balance. When he finally saw her standing in the doorway, he held out his arms and she ran into them.

"Is it true? Are you sure?" he asked.

"I'm sure."

"How sure?"

"Very sure," she said, laughing. "For goodness sake! So sure, in fact, that I've put in for a temporary transfer back to Reservations until after the baby is born."

"Charlotte," he said. "But your job. And Venice. When are you going to go to Venice? It's what you've always wanted."

"No, Pruitt," she said. "You are what I've always wanted. I may not have always realized it, but it's the truth you've helped me to find. All those other things, those dreams that I thought could replace love in my life, that I thought might fulfill me in the same way, what I've found is that they're just journeys I want to take. When I stand them up next to you, and to this baby growing inside me . . . nothing can take the place of that. Nothing is more important than love."

"We'll plan a trip right away," he decided. "We'll tour Italy. Can you do that while you're pregnant? Because I don't see any reason why you can't have it all, Charlotte. I really don't."

"Oh, Seth."

They kissed so tenderly that something flopped over inside Charlotte's stomach.

"What!" Seth cried when she reacted. "What is it?"

"It's your baby, all right, Pruitt. It's kicking me with those big old scuffed shoes!"

"Isn't it a little early for kicking?" he asked innocently.

"Right," she replied with a toss of her head, "and everything we do is always in such perfect timing."